THE NURSE'S REUNION WISH

CAROL MARINELLI

MILLS & BOON

First published in Great Britain 2020
by Mills & Boon, an imprint of HarperCollins*Publishers*
1 London Bridge Street, London, SE1 9GF

Large Print edition 2020

ISBN: 978-0-263-08592-1

MIX
Paper from responsible sources
FSC™ C007454

This book is produced from independently certified FSC™ paper to ensure responsible forest management. For more information visit www.harpercollins.co.uk/green.

Printed and bound in Great Britain
by CPI Group (UK) Ltd, Croydon, CR0 4YY

Carol Marinelli recently filled in a form asking for her job title. Thrilled to be able to put down her answer, she put 'writer'. Then it asked what Carol did for relaxation and she put down the truth—'writing'. The third question asked for her hobbies. Well, not wanting to look obsessed, she crossed her fingers and answered 'swimming'—but, given that the chlorine in the pool does terrible things to her highlights, I'm sure you can guess the real answer!

Also by Carol Marinelli

Playboy on Her Christmas List
Their Secret Royal Baby
Their One Night Baby
The Midwife's One-Night Fling
The Sicilian's Surprise Love-Child
Secret Prince's Christmas Seduction

Ruthless Royal Sheikhs miniseries

Captive for the Sheikh's Pleasure
Christmas Bride for the Sheikh

Discover more at millsandboon.co.uk.

For Hannah and Ben
Love you guys
Carol xxxx

CHAPTER ONE

SOME WOULD SAY that Rachel Walker had a superpower.

She was an emergency nurse, slight of build, and looked younger than her thirty-two years, which wasn't much of an advantage. With her fiery red hair and porcelain skin it might be expected that she would blush easily. But Rachel's pale skin rarely flushed. As well as that, her huge green eyes revealed little of her thoughts even as she held someone's gaze.

And while that might not sound like much of a superpower, when a patient was critically ill and terrified, or revealing his innermost troubles, it rather helped that the emergency nurse remained outwardly calm and seemingly unfazed.

Rachel had long ago learnt to hide her deepest feelings.

Growing up in Sheffield, in a loud, happy

family, with gregarious parents and four older brothers, she had found it necessary, from an early age, to retain a neutral expression and not let anyone reap the effects of their persistent, albeit good-natured, teasing.

But then, aged six, Rachel had come home from school to a house full of aunts and uncles, neighbours and family friends and found out that her mother had suddenly died. The teasing had stopped and the laughter had faded from the Walker home, and the little girl had quickly discovered that her dad and her brothers could not deal with her grief and tears.

'Take her to the park,' Dad would say when she cried for her mum.

Rachel had duly been taken to the park and pushed on a swing, or spun on a roundabout, or bumped up and down on a seesaw until her brothers had been satisfied that she'd return home smiling, at least for a little while.

The tears would soon start again, of course.

Especially at night, when she'd missed her mum tucking her up in bed and reading her bedtime stories, or when she would wake from a dream calling out for her.

'Come on now, Rachel,' her dad would tell her. 'You're upsetting our Phil with your carry-on.'

When she'd cried one day at school, and they'd had to call her dad to come from work to pick her up *again*, she'd known her tears were causing real problems. Her dad owned his own removal company and, as he'd explained that afternoon, people relied on him to get the job done.

'It's their moving day, Rachel,' he said as she sat in the front of his lorry. 'If I have to be called away, who's going to move them into their new house? And what about the family that are waiting to move in to theirs? You've got them thinking they'll have nowhere to sleep tonight. Now, stop with them tears and be a good girl.'

Then one day it had been 'our Phil' himself who had warned her. 'Enough now, Rachel! Dad doesn't need to hear it. He's upset enough and missing Mum too. You're just making things worse.'

Finally Rachel had stopped with the tears and the questions about her mum. Her emotions hadn't stopped, of course—she'd just learnt to hide them.

This superpower she now possessed hadn't done much for her relationships, but on this cold February morning, in the Emergency Department of London's Primary Hospital, even though Rachel had only worked there for a week, her particular skill had been recognised.

She had been assigned to the minor injuries unit and was helping a young man with crutches when the intercom buzzed and she heard her name being called by May, the unit manager.

'Excuse me a moment,' Rachel said. But, reluctant to leave the man wobbling, she just went and stood by the curtains, so she could keep an eye on him as she answered the call.

'Yes?'

'Can I ask you to come down to Resus?'

'Sure,' Rachel said. 'I'll just—'

'Immediately.'

As May summoned her, the chimes went off and the request for an anaesthetist to go to the ED went out.

Rachel called over her shoulder to a colleague to come and take over with the young man. Then she made her way through the department, via Reception and the central waiting room, which was particularly full, and through to the main section of the unit, where she could see May standing outside the resuscitation area looking in.

Rachel liked her new unit manager. She was caring in the way of a mother hen, but also wise and sharp.

May gestured for Rachel to stand with her and observe as she told her about the patient. 'Thomas Jennings, eighteen-month-old with query epiglottitis, just arrived in the department. Mother drove him here…thought he had croup.'

Even from this distance Rachel could see that Thomas was a very sick little boy indeed. He sat on his mother's knee, leaning forward and drooling, his breathing noisy and laboured. She could hear the stridor—a high-pitched wheezing—from outside the room.

'Where is everyone?' Rachel asked, because she could only see Tara, a fellow RN, in there.

'Jordan the paediatrician is here,' May explained. 'He's on the phone, out of earshot of Mum, trying to get hold of an anaesthetist. But the on-call team are up on ITU and the second team is in Theatre.'

Sure enough, as soon as May said that the chimes went off again, summoning an anaesthetist to the resuscitation area of the ED.

Epiglottitis could quickly turn life-threatening. It was an inflammation of the flap of cartilage and mucous membrane at the back of the throat that guarded the windpipe. Thanks to immunisation, it was now rarely seen. Still, at any moment little Thomas's airway could become obstructed—hence the need for an anaesthetist to be present.

'Mum's getting upset that we're not doing anything and Tara's getting a bit flustered,' May explained, and then glanced at Rachel, who stood there unruffled, taking it all in.

She must have looked so calm that May felt she had to double-check that she understood the precariousness of the situation.

'You *do* know how quickly a patient with epiglottitis can deteriorate?'

'Yes, May,' Rachel answered calmly. 'Has everything been set up for a tracheostomy?'

'That's why I called for you to come down,' May admitted. 'I'll leave you to it. I'm staying back, so as not to distress the little man with too many people around him, but I'll be hovering should you need me.'

'Thanks,' Rachel said, glad to know that May was near as she walked into the room.

'Morning.' Rachel smiled at both Tara and the mother, but she didn't fuss over the little boy.

His blond hair was dark with sweat and plastered to his head, and he buried his face in his mum's chest at the sight of a new arrival.

The monitors were all turned up and bleeping loudly. Rachel turned the volume down—given all the staff who were close by—doing what she could to make the surroundings less scary.

'He's never been in hospital before,' Mrs Jennings said.

'It's very overwhelming.' Rachel nodded. 'But you're doing great. I know it looks as if we're not doing much, but the most important thing right now is to keep Thomas from getting upset.'

'Where's the anaesthetist?' Mrs Jennings asked, her voice rising in panic.

'On the way,' Rachel said, privately hoping that was the case.

Tara spoke then. 'I was just explaining to Mum that if we can get a couple of local anaesthetic patches onto Thomas it would be a great help when we cannulate him.'

'Good idea—but perhaps Mum could do it,' Rachel suggested, and then looked over to Mrs Jennings. 'I'll show you how.'

There probably wouldn't be time for the cream to take effect before he was cannulated, but hopefully it would save him a little pain and distress, which was the main goal here.

Thomas didn't flinch as his mother copied Rachel's instructions and the patches were applied, which concerned Rachel greatly.

She glanced over to Tara. 'Has everything been set up for the transfer?'

'I was just about to do that,' Tara said.

Thomas had only been in the department for ten minutes, but things had to be moved along speedily, as the situation could change at any minute. And it was starting to. He was becoming increasingly exhausted, and Rachel knew she had to get everything they might possibly need on a trolley as quickly as possible.

'I'm going to get things ready for Thomas's transfer,' Rachel said to the mum, 'but I'll be right here.'

All seemed calm.

All was not.

Outside the room there was a flurry of activity taking place. The paediatrician was alerting the operating theatre, and the anaesthetist, who had just arrived in the hospital and collected his pager, was sprinting down the long corridor towards the ED. Rachel was preparing the trolley, and outside May was calling Security to clear the corridor and hold the lifts while the transfer was made.

It was imperative that the little boy did not become distressed, so the staff were hands-off, leaving it to his mother to comfort him as they hovered discreetly and prepared for the worst.

Rachel started to collect the equipment

they would need for the transfer while keeping an eye on Thomas. She glanced out and saw Jordan on the phone, running a worried hand through his hair, but he plastered on a smile when he returned from his call and gave Rachel a nod, then made small talk with Mrs Jennings about his own three children while keeping a very close eye on Thomas.

'There's Nicholas, who is Thomas's age,' Jordan said, 'and the twins are three—'

His words halted as the doors slid open.

'Ah, the anaesthetist is here, Mrs Jennings. This is Dr Hadley.'

Hadley?

Rachel glanced over towards the doors at the sound of the familiar name. And the world as she knew it changed as Dominic Hadley stepped in.

Rachel quickly turned back to the trolley she was preparing, drawing in a deep breath when she suddenly felt giddy.

Dominic Hadley worked at The Primary?

Dominic was a doctor?

An anaesthetist?

How?

When?

Though his voice was slightly breathless from running, it was a deeper and more assured voice than the one she had known. As he spoke with Jordan, Rachel screwed her eyes tightly shut, for she did not know how to face him. How to turn around and deal with this situation?

Because it really was a situation.

Dominic Hadley had hurt her badly.

So badly that it had taken her more than a decade to recover her heart enough to try to love again.

So badly that as she stood there anger, hurt and recrimination fought for first place in the order of her feelings.

But she could not think of that here, so she focused on the soft bleeps of Thomas's monitors and forced the surge of animosity within her to settle. She wondered about Dominic's reaction when he saw her.

Dominic had not a clue.

Yet.

'I'm just going to let Richard know,' Dominic told Jordan. 'Though I'm not sure if he's in ye—'

His voice halted as a flash of red hair caught his eye and he couldn't help but check the profile of the nurse who was preparing to transfer Thomas up to Theatre.

It happened every now and then—a glimpse of red hair would make him turn his head, or the sound of laughter in a bar would have him scanning the crowd—but then he would remind himself that there hadn't been much laughter at the end of their relationship.

But it couldn't be Rachel, Dominic thought, and dismissed her from his mind as Jordan continued to bring him up to speed.

'Mrs Jennings understands that we won't examine Thomas until we're safely in Theatre, and she's consented to a tracheostomy, should it be necessary.'

Dominic looked over to the anxious woman, who was doing all she could to hold it together for the sake of her son.

'Hello, I'm Dominic Hadley—the anaesthetic registrar.' He gave her a smile, but noted that the little boy whimpered at the rather imposing sight of him so halted his approach. He stood a couple of inches over six foot and, sharply dressed in a navy suit, he was aware he might look rather imposing, so he sat down on the resuscitation bed a little further away from Thomas. 'What would you like me to call you?' he asked.

'Please,' Mrs Jennings said, 'call me Haylee.'

'And do you understand what's happening, Haylee?'

She gave a helpless shrug. 'Not really. The children's doctor said he might need to be put on a breathing machine, and an airway made in his neck…'

'It's called a tracheostomy.' Dominic nodded.

Time was of the essence, but so was explanation. He drew a rudimentary picture of a throat on the pad he carried in his pocket.

'The epiglottis is a flap of tissue at the back of the throat. If that swells so much that we can't get a tube past it, then an incision would need to be made here.' He pointed to the picture he'd drawn and then to the same spot on his own throat. 'That way we can bypass the swelling.'

'But he might not have to have one?'

'We won't know till we look at Thomas's

throat. I'd prefer to do that in Theatre, where we can examine him properly and get treatment underway. I'll attempt to secure his airway, though a tracheostomy might well be the only course available to us.'

Haylee looked down at the picture and then to her son, who was working very hard to breathe.

Dominic was deeply concerned and he would feel a lot better if they were in Theatre. 'Thomas really needs antibiotics and IV fluids,' he said. 'But putting in a cannula is only going to upset him, so the very best thing we can do is get him up to Theatre and take care of everything there.'

'I understand that,' said Haylee Jennings as she cuddled her son.

'Have you got anyone here with you?'

'My husband's on his way.'

'Good,' Dominic said. 'I'm just going to let my senior know what's happening and...'

He glanced up to let the nurse know they'd be heading up to Theatre imminently, and it was then that Dominic realised he hadn't been wrong at all.

The nurse was Rachel.

It helped, as an anaesthetist, to have nerves of steel. For Dominic, it was an acquired trait. Some called him arrogant, but those nerves of steel were invaluable now that he was faced with this unlikely situation.

Dominic looked through Rachel, rather than at her.

In fact, Dominic barely blinked.

'We'll head up shortly,' he informed her. 'I'm going to make a quick call first.'

'Ready when you are,' Rachel replied, in a voice that was both measured and calm.

Yes, a superpower indeed!

As Dominic Hadley selected some drugs and syringes from the cart and stalked off, there was a moment when Rachel wondered if he'd even recognised her.

After all, she'd barely recognised *him*!

There was little about this polished, suave man who commanded the room that compared with the awkward physics geek she had fallen in love with.

Although his thick black hair was the same, still damp from his morning shower, and the soapy male scent of him was familiar. His dark eyes were the same gorgeous velvet brown as they had always been too. He had always towered above her, but he seemed taller now, if that were possible. And he had definitely broadened out, and looked immaculate in his sharp navy suit, pale blue shirt and lilac tie.

Her dad, if he were here, would probably say it was pink…

What sort of man wears a pink tie? Rachel could almost hear her father's thick Yorkshire accent.

With the phone pressed between his ear and his shoulder, Dominic pulled up the drugs he might need, should there be an emergency en route, as he let his boss know the situation.

'Any history?' asked Richard Lewis, the consultant anaesthetist.

'Unvaccinated.' Dominic clipped back his response. But his voice faltered as he glanced over to Resus, where Rachel still stood. There was a whole lot of history right there…

'Healthy little boy until this morning, nil allergies…' He went through the case, and it was agreed that Richard, who was currently on ITU, would meet him up in Theatre.

'We're heading straight up,' Dominic told May as he replaced the phone.

'They're ready for you. Rachel will come up to Theatre with you.'

Dominic felt as if his heart might pump its way up to his throat and wondered if it would be better to object to Rachel escorting him.

'She's new. I need someone who knows what they're doing.'

'Which is why I'm sending Rachel. She might be new but she's worked in Paediatric Emergency up in Sheffield and is very competent.'

'Fine.' He walked over to the cooler and filled a little plastic cup with water, drained it, filled it again, drained it again, and told himself to remove Rachel from his mind entirely. He headed back in, determined to ignore the fact that Rachel had just dropped back into his life.

For now.

'We're going to get Thomas up to Theatre now,' Dominic informed Haylee. 'We'll put you in a wheelchair, with Thomas on your knee, but if there's an emergency on the way, then we've got everything we need to deal with it.'

Rachel—or rather, he told himself, *the nurse*—helped mother and child into the wheelchair as he ran a knowing eye along the equipment she had prepared for the journey.

'Ready?' Dominic checked as Rachel wrapped a blanket around Thomas and his mum.

'Ready,' *the nurse* agreed and gave the mother a smile…

Except it was Rachel's smile, and to Dominic it felt like a punch in the guts. It was summer and spring all rolled into one. It was the memory of Saturday nights watching a movie while eating a curry in bed. It was a forgotten ten-pound note found in her jeans that she'd waved over her head before taking him for breakfast in the café across the street.

But he was determined that her smile would not be his undoing.

'Ready,' Jordan said.

There was a blast of cold air as they left the department and he tried not to notice Rachel briefly rub her bare arms.

It was a reminder for Dominic that Rachel was always cold—and not just in body temperature. He'd never been allowed inside that head of hers, so he did all he could to put her out of his now.

It was a very long walk up the corridor. Rachel's eyes never left Thomas's face as Haylee nervously chatted away. 'I thought he had croup,' she admitted. 'But he was blue when I went to him…'

'Well, he's in the right place now,' Rachel said, doing her level best to keep Haylee as calm as she could.

'Have you worked here long?' Haylee asked.

'I've only been here a week,' Rachel admitted. 'Before that I worked in a paediatric emergency department in Sheffield.'

'I thought I heard a northern accent.' Haylee nodded and looked up at Rachel. 'Do you have any children?'

'No,' Rachel said.

To her utter, aching regret, the answer *was* no, even if it wasn't strictly true. But it was much easier just to say no and deny her son's existence than to walk along a corridor with someone she didn't know and admit to the agony.

'No, I don't.'

The porters were holding the lift for them, and as the group got in, Rachel gave them a nod of thanks, relieved that attention could be diverted from her answer to Haylee's question.

The lift doors closed and Haylee looked up at Jordan. 'So, you've got three children?'

'I do,' Jordan said. 'All boys.'

Rachel held her breath as Haylee asked Dominic the same question. 'What about you, Doctor?'

How would Dominic respond?

For Rachel, worse than having him reveal their past would be hearing about his present. Was she about to learn that he was married with two little ones or one on the way?

As she awaited his response, Rachel found she was holding her breath. Was she going to have to hide her reaction to hearing about a Mrs Hadley? Or a soon-to-be Mrs Hadley? And how would she react to that?

* * *

Dominic wasn't about to enlighten anyone.

He would rather be anywhere than in this lift right now. And *this* morning, of all mornings, it was imperative that he keep his private and professional worlds firmly separated.

'I try not to bring my personal life to work, Haylee,' he said, and let out a steadying breath. 'It makes it easier for me to focus.'

Haylee nodded and gave a small smile, not offended in the least at the slight rebuff, and he saw Rachel let go of the breath she'd been holding.

The lift swished them to the second floor, and they were soon gliding along the highly polished corridor and into the controlled world of the operating theatre, where more medical staff awaited them.

'Stay with him,' Dominic ordered Rachel. 'A familiar face might help.'

But Rachel's familiar face most certainly wasn't helping Dominic, so it was Thomas Jennings he kept on his mind as he went off to change into scrubs.

* * *

As the theatre nurses checked Thomas's ID, and ran through questions with his mum, Richard Lewis came in and introduced himself.

Jordan was ordering an IV and drugs, but the efficient theatre staff were taking care of that, and Rachel again found that she felt a little giddy.

Not in an about-to-faint way. Just giddy from the heat of Theatre, she tried to convince herself. Of course she was worried about Thomas, but mostly she was overwhelmed by seeing Dominic again—but she never let it show, not even for a second. Even when Dominic returned, dressed in scrubs and a theatre cap, she gave him as banal a look as she could muster.

'Let's get a line in,' Dominic said, and then added to Rachel, 'Can you try to distract him?'

The numbing gel had only recently been applied, but she hoped it would take the edge off the cannula going in. More important, Thomas was increasingly cyanosed and becoming rather listless, so it was imperative they moved quickly.

Haylee cuddled her son while Dominic eased a cannula into his little vein.

'Good boy,' Dominic said when it was all done and hooked up.

Now that IV access had been secured, it was time for Rachel to escort Thomas's mum out of the operating theatre. But before she left, Dominic caught the tearful woman's eye. 'I won't leave his side,' he said.

'Thank you,' Haylee said.

She turned and waved as her son let out a raspy cry, but allowed Rachel to lead her out.

'They'll take the very best care of him,' Rachel said.

'That anaesthetist—he seems to know what he's doing,' Haylee said as Rachel led her to the relatives' room. 'Thomas will be safe with him.'

'Yes,' Rachel said. 'Dr Hadley will take the very best care.'

It was a difficult intubation. Thomas's throat was swollen, and the vocal cords were hard to visualise, but with Richard's quiet and reassuring presence, Dominic got the tube in and thankfully a tracheostomy wasn't necessary. Swabs and bloods were taken, and antibiotics and IV fluids were started.

Thomas was moved over to the ITU, where, sedated and ventilated, his little body could finally start to fight the infection, and it wasn't long before Haylee was allowed to return to her son's side. Only then did Dominic leave him.

'Well done,' Richard said as Dominic took a seat at the nurses' station that looked out over the whole of ITU and pulled up Thomas's incoming blood work on the computer.

'Thanks.'

Richard turned his head at this rather muted response from Dominic. He noted the pallor on his colleague's face, and saw that his usually suave registrar was suddenly anything but.

'Is everything okay?' Richard checked.

'Not really,' he admitted, and ran a hand over his forehead now that the surprising turn of events had begun to sink in. 'There's a nurse down in Emergency…'

Richard rolled his eyes. This happened all

too often where Dominic was concerned. 'You need to learn to let them down more gently,' Richard suggested.

But Dominic was silent.

He knew it would be far more sensible to say nothing. To just let it go.

After all, what had happened between him and Rachel had been more than a decade ago.

Way more than a decade.

It had been thirteen years, in fact.

Yes, better to stay silent, Dominic decided.

Except the shock of the morning had been so great—or maybe it was just that he couldn't hold it in any longer—that he told his senior the truth.

'It's not like that,' Dominic said, for it wasn't a little glitch with an ex or some disgruntled lover that was troubling him.

Rachel had been way more than that.

'I just ran into my ex-wife.'

CHAPTER TWO

'EX-WIFE?' RICHARD did a double-take, perhaps thinking he had misheard or that Dominic was joking.

'Yes.'

'Your ex-wife is working in Emergency? You never said you'd been married. I had no idea.'

How could he have? Dominic thought to himself. Apart from a fleeting conversation with Jordan and his wife, a couple of years ago, he'd never discussed his brief marriage with anyone. To Dominic's colleagues, friends—and lovers—he was the personification of an eternal playboy bachelor.

'It was a long time ago,' Dominic clipped, already regretting saying anything. 'It didn't last for long.'

'What happened?' Richard persisted.

'We were young.' Dominic shrugged and

turned back to the computer. 'We got married for all the wrong reasons.'

'Such as?'

But Dominic wasn't going to answer that one.

'We both agreed it was a mistake. I haven't seen her in…' He blew out a sigh. 'Years.'

'And how does it feel to see her now?'

Dominic thought for a moment. How *did* it feel to see Rachel again?

Challenging.

It felt as if every mistake he had ever made in life was suddenly being paraded in front of him, but he played it down to his boss.

'Surprised. I never thought she'd leave Sheffield,' Dominic admitted, but he deliberately didn't offer her name, nor let on that it was Rachel. There were always staff coming and going at The Primary, and he was quietly relieved Richard hadn't picked up on the tension between them this morning. 'She's all about her family.'

'What are they like?' Richard asked.

'Her mum died, so there's just her dad—and she's ever so protective of him. Oh, and there are four hulking brothers. They're all very parochial…' His voice trailed off. He didn't mean it in a derogatory way, but as an outsider it had been impossible to break in to their clique. 'They considered me weak.'

'Weak?' Richard frowned, clearly non-plussed, because Dominic, as well as being tall and broad-shouldered, was incredibly confident and assured.

'A bit of a pansy,' Dominic elaborated. 'And I guess I was back then.'

Richard laughed, but it faded when he saw the serious expression on his colleague's face.

'What was your wife like?'

'Tricky,' Dominic said—which was the understatement of the year.

But he really didn't want to discuss it, so when his pager buzzed he pounced on it and saw that it was Maternity.

'*Your* wife is paging me,' Dominic said, and gave a wry smile. Richard's wife, Freya, was a midwife, and had just started back at work after the birth of their son William. 'I'm needed over in Maternity for an epidural.'

But Richard had more to say on the topic of

Dominic's ex-wife. 'I can go and give the epidural. Why don't you go and speak with…?'

Richard was waiting, Dominic guessed, for him to offer a name, but he would not be revealing that.

'It must have been a big shock for your ex-wife too,' Richard said.

'She seemed fine with it.' Dominic shrugged.

Only, he knew that couldn't be true. Rachel buried her emotions deep, and he had been denied access to them right from the start. When they'd first got together he had asked about her mother, wondering how her loss at such an early age had affected Rachel, but she had shut him down. And then, in those final painful days when he'd tried to speak to her about their son, Rachel had made it very clear she did not want him to get close.

Well, she'd got her wish, and although it appeared they might be working together for the foreseeable future, they had never been further apart.

'*I'll* head up to Maternity,' he said.

'No, no.' Richard stood and pulled rank. 'I'm going. There's a patient with COPD down in Emergency. He needs a pre-op assessment. Could you go and take care of that, please?'

Dominic's jaw gritted.

'And while you're there perhaps you could manage a conversation with your ex-wife, to ensure that you're both okay with the situation?'

'We'll be fine.'

'Good. Then you'll have no issue heading down to Emergency.'

'Of course I won't. But as for having a conversation with my ex-wife, there's nothing left to talk about,' Dominic said. 'It was all said and done with years ago.'

Not really.

There had been an awful lot left unsaid.

Rachel had walked back down towards the Emergency Department in somewhat of a daze. She had been completely unprepared to see him and felt utterly sideswiped.

Her move to London was still so new. Of course she knew that Dominic was from here, so she'd been braced to run into him on the street, or in a shop or café, even while telling herself she was being ridiculous—

after all, there were more than eight million people living in London.

Not for a second had she expected to see him at work.

A doctor?

An anaesthetist!

When?

He wasn't exactly a people person. In fact, the Dominic she'd known had been rather socially awkward. The Dominic she'd known had had one interest—physics—and had been determined that one day he'd be a research scientist. He'd been heading off to university for just that purpose.

Okay, he'd had *two* interests, Rachel amended as she opened the large double doors to Emergency: physics and sex.

She dared not allow herself to think of the latter, though!

'How's Thomas?' May pounced the second Rachel returned to the department.

'I'm not sure,' Rachel said. 'I took Mum over to the ITU relatives' room, but Thomas was still in Theatre when I left.'

'I'll call them in a little while,' May said.

Rachel looked over to May, who was writing on the whiteboard as she chatted, and oddly found that she wanted to confide in her.

May, she wanted to say, *how long has Dominic Hadley worked here?* Or, *May, that registrar anaesthetist—well, he just happens to be my ex-husband and I don't know quite what to do.*

But Rachel said nothing.

'Are you okay to go back to work in Minor Injuries?' May asked, taking her glasses off and smiling at Rachel.

'Sure.'

'Would you mind restocking Resus first?' May directed a slight eye-roll at Tara. 'You know what you used.'

Restocking was tedious, but essential—especially in Resus. It was imperative that all the equipment was exactly where it should be when it was needed the most.

A lot of the packs had been opened, though not necessarily used, so there was a lot of replacing and reordering to do. Rachel did so methodically, glad of the chance to get better acquainted with the area.

Tara was taking care of an elderly patient

who'd had a seizure. He was currently sleeping while they awaited his transfer to a ward. She joined Rachel in Resus.

'How long did you work in Emergency in Sheffield?' she asked as Rachel replaced the oxygen tubing and mask and checked the suction.

'Three years in Emergency all up. I did hairdressing before I went into nursing.'

They chatted lightly as Rachel worked, though Rachel's heart wasn't really in the conversation. She was still reeling from seeing Dominic that morning, and wondering how on earth they would be with each other when they eventually spoke.

The patient Tara was caring for was soon transferred, so she came and gave Rachel a hand, both of them checking the intubation tray's contents before sealing it up.

'Keep an eye on Dominic,' Tara said suddenly.

'Sorry?' Rachel blinked.

'Dominic Hadley—the registrar anaesthetist. I saw him looking at you when he was on the phone.'

Rachel decided it was best to act vague. 'What do you mean?'

'I'm just trying to give you a heads-up. Dominic might best be described as "nice while it lasts"—but, believe me, it never does.'

Rachel could hear the bitterness in Tara's voice. It was clear there was history between her and Dominic, and from the sound of things, he had become a bit of a player. It was all just so at odds with the man she had once known.

She wondered what Tara's reaction would be if she told her she had once been married to him, and decided there and then that her and Dominic's past would *not* be joining them at The Primary.

There was no way she wanted the fact they'd been married to get out. And aside from that…

'I'm engaged,' Rachel said, 'and even if I weren't…'

She left it there, because it felt safer to do so than to let her imagination wander down *that* track.

No way!

Her heart had been placed under lock and key after she and Dominic had broken up. It had taken years for her to forge another relationship. There had been a couple of cursory attempts at dating, but they hadn't worked out. And then, when she'd first started working in Emergency, she'd met Gordon, a friend of her flatmate, who was kind and made her feel safe.

When the accounting firm he worked for had offered him a promotion that had required him to move to London, Gordon had asked her to join him. It had felt like a big leap to agree to live with him, on top of moving cities and jobs for him, but the night before they'd left for London Gordon had, at the leaving party her dad had thrown for them, asked her to marry him. And now they were engaged.

Not that she wore her ring to work.

With the restock done, Rachel signed off and headed back to the minor injuries section. But an hour or so later, unable to concentrate and desperate for a moment's peace, she said she was going to find her cardigan and made her way to the changing rooms.

Without even bothering to switch on the light, Rachel sat on the bench in semi-darkness, the sounds of the Emergency Department muffled behind the thick door, and put her head in her hands, trying to process things.

Dominic was a doctor.

That nerdy teenager she had known was now a sharp-suited anaesthetist with something of a reputation with women, given it had taken all of one moment in his presence to be warned of his ways.

Despite keeping her head down, the giddy feeling refused to abate—and then Rachel suddenly recognised what the feeling was: it was how she had always felt when she was with him.

Yes, Dominic Hadley made her giddy—and had done so from the very first day they had met.

It had been September, and both had been starting their last year of senior school. His father, a professor, had accepted a role at the university in Sheffield, and the family had moved up there and enrolled Dominic in a top school.

Rachel had been there on a hard-won scholarship, and had never really fitted in, while Dominic had been sent there as a matter of course.

Not that he'd wanted to be there.

He had missed London and his old school friends.

Despite being from very different backgrounds, they had struck up a friendship. They had both been complete geeks.

She'd had braces, and Dominic had just had his ceramic ones taken off, so on the very first day of their final school year their first conversation had been about the importance of retainers.

'Get two sets made,' Dominic had advised her, 'and wear them every night.' He'd told her about a friend in London who hadn't worn his and now was having to start all over again.

'Oh, I'll wear them.' Rachel had nodded and smiled her silver-and-elastic-band NHS smile. 'I won't be able to afford them once I turn eighteen.'

They had both been very serious about their schoolwork and the conversation had turned to chemistry, which she had found impossible but he'd handled with ease.

'Do you want me to help you?' he'd offered when, halfway through the first term, she'd found herself falling behind. 'We could go through some things after school?'

He had written his address down on her exercise book and that same afternoon she had made her way to his house.

His mother's smile had been tight when she'd greeted Rachel. Professor Hadley hadn't even attempted one, and had made it clear he was less than impressed by his son's choice of friend.

'You have homework of your own to do, Dominic.'

It had been obvious to Rachel that she wasn't particularly welcome in the Hadley household, so he had started to come to her little terraced home after school.

'What time does your mum get home?' Dominic had asked that first time, as they'd made tea and found biscuits in the kitchen.

'There's just my dad and my brothers, and they usually get in around seven.'

'Where's your mum?' Dominic asked.

'She's dead.'

'Rachel!'

He sounded stunned, and waited for her to elaborate, but she knew that if she explained further she would break down, and her tears had long since been removed from this house.

'I'm so sorry.'

'It's fine,' she said, picking up her mug and heading up the stairs to her room, hoping he would leave things there.

Except he did not.

'How?' Dominic asked as he followed her up. 'When?'

But Rachel reminded him that he had come over so they could study together. There should be no more to it than that.

Except those walks to her home through the park started to stretch for longer. The same park where she'd been spun and swung as a child. Sometimes they'd take a seat on the park bench, or lie on the grass and talk as they gazed up at the sky.

About the clouds.

About other kids in their class.

About their studies and how he liked coming to her home. He told her that his parents fought *a lot*.

'Badly?' Rachel asked, and turned to look at his tense expression as he nodded.

'We moved up here so they could have a fresh start,' Dominic told her. 'He had an affair.'

'Oh.' Rachel was unused to such candour.

'But it sounds as if it's still going on,' Dominic said. 'I don't know why she stays with him when he makes her so miserable.' He looked over to her then. 'Do you think your dad will ever get a girlfriend?'

'No!' Rachel gave a soft laugh at the very thought. 'He says he's got enough going on with the five of us.'

Dominic turned and looked at her. 'How *did* your mother die?'

There was gentleness in his enquiry. He rolled from his back onto his side, and then, leaning on his elbow, he looked down at her, and she looked up into dark eyes that wanted to know her better.

And, given what he'd just shared about his parents, she told him the little she could without crying. 'Something ruptured in her brain.'

'Was it sudden?'

'Very.'

'Do you miss her?'

Every day, she wanted to say, but she was so scared at the depth of her feelings that she didn't know how to share them.

'I don't really remember her,' Rachel said instead, because that was sort of true as well.

She remembered some things—like her smile and her kiss, and lying in bed listening to a story; the soft lilt of her Irish voice and the sparkle of her ring as she turned the page, her pretty red nails as she pointed to words, how safe she had felt when wrapped in her perfumed arms.

But she knew she'd cry if she told him that.

And so she didn't.

Sometimes Rachel would turn her head just for a quiet gaze at Dominic. The more time she spent with him, the more *aware* of him she became, all the while telling herself it could never be.

So she hid how she felt, because that was the only way she knew how to live.

'I never know what you're thinking,' Dominic said late one afternoon as he met her cool green gaze.

She was about to respond that she was thinking about the equation he'd just put in front of her, but that wouldn't be true. She could feel the warmth from his thigh next to hers, and when their heads bent forward over a book she ached with the effort of not turning her face to his.

So now she did.

His gaze was intense, with an expression she had never seen before. For once it felt as if he could see her hidden desire, and yet she did not look away.

'Perhaps I don't want you to know,' she said.

'Can I at least try and guess?'

'You can try.'

'And if I'm wrong?' Dominic checked. 'Will we still be friends?'

'We'll still be—'

Her voice had been halted by the softness of his lips against hers. Dominic's guess had been absolutely right. Because of course she'd been dreaming of his kiss since the first day they'd met.

In her bedroom, sitting at her desk, he kissed her soft and slow, and she forgot about her braces, and she forgot about her inexperience, because he was new to this too.

And they were no longer shy.

No longer awkward.

At least not when it was just the two of them.

Together they revised for their looming exams, and together they learned about themselves and each other. And Rachel's braces came off, but thanks to Dominic, she felt beautiful way before then.

It wasn't all plain sailing, though.

His parents didn't approve of their friendship, so they worked hard to hide their blossoming romance.

And *her* father, who usually got on with everyone, took an instant dislike to the awkward, polite, private school boy who, to top it all off, was from down south.

Even her brothers chimed in with less-than-sage advice.

'Don't be letting him know you like him, Rachel.'

'You have to play hard to get, Rachel.'

'He's using you, Rachel. Just stay well back.'

But nothing—not warnings, nor dire predictions, no force on this earth—could stop them.

There was secret hand-holding under desks, and stolen kisses despite the open bedroom door her dad insisted on.

And there were forbidden touches in the times when they found themselves alone…

They always made sure, though, that when Rachel's dad or brothers dropped home unannounced to check on them they would find two nerdy teenagers really studying that science.

One day Dominic decreed that Rachel had to get ninety per cent on a practice test if she wanted a reward. Since she only managed eighty-eight per cent, even with his generous marking, he refused to allow her any prize.

'Sorry, Rachel…' He gave her a sad smile. 'You failed. Back to work!'

And back to the textbook she went—until

the rattle of the removals lorry rumbling up the hilly narrow street where Rachel lived announced the arrival of her family.

'We're about to be checked on...' Dominic sighed.

'Good.' Rachel smiled in utter relief—because the sooner they were checked on, the sooner they'd be left alone again.

The front door crashed open and Phil ran up the stairs.

'Dad forgot his...' Phil stopped at the top of the stairs and saw the two of them deep in their books. 'Oh, hi, there, Dominic. Didn't know you were coming over...'

'I told Dad he would be,' Rachel said indignantly.

'Hello.' Dominic gave his usual awkward smile. 'How are you, Phil?'

'Grand. So, what are the two of you doing?'

'Revising.' Rachel rolled her eyes.

'Oh.'

They actually were. There were books, pencils, tea and biscuits, and not a single untoward thing had taken place.

'I'll leave you to it, then.'

The removals lorry rattled its noisy way

down the steep road as Dominic totted up Rachel's latest score.

Ninety-two per cent!

He'd slammed the book closed and she'd lain on her bed with her skirt up and closed her eyes in the bliss he gave.

'There…' she would moan needlessly. 'There!'

And *there* he would flick with his tongue, over and over.

And *there* he would ignore a moment later, as he buried his face deep into her.

And she would press her mouth to the inside of her elbow and try not to scream his name.

'Dominic, Dominic, Dominic!'

And then, deliciously, he had to have the same. And each kiss, each intimate touch, each climax they gave to each other, led them to want more, more, *more*.

They had both been virgins. The first time they'd tried her dad and brothers had been on a removal the other side of town—a big job that would see them there every day for a week. So, on that cold but sunny November morning, they had finally, properly, been alone.

It had been an unmitigated disaster.

Rachel had bled and felt sick because it had hurt so much, and Dominic had finished before they'd barely started.

Yes, a serious disaster.

Embarrassing and awkward didn't even begin to describe it.

Never again, they'd both fervently agreed.

Never, *ever* again.

Absolutely not.

Dominic had arrived for their usual study session the next day. It had been pouring with rain. He'd shaken off his dad's golf umbrella in the little porch, and with a lot of residual blushing and awkwardness, they'd resumed their studies…

Despite the umbrella, his damp hair had dripped on the page as the rain beat on the window, and when they'd kissed, they'd matched again. The pressure of their attempt the day before had fallen away as easily as their clothing.

She'd felt as if she were drowning in his

kisses, and at his touch, as if she were floating across the sky…

Their second time had been sublime.

That had been their first winter. And as spring had inched towards summer, and they'd lain on her little single bed, naked and sated, Rachel had made an admission.

'I'm going to miss our study sessions when we're at university.'

Dominic was hoping to study physics at St Andrews in Scotland, or at Imperial College in London, whereas Rachel wanted to do midwifery in Sheffield.

'What are you talking about?' Dominic asked. 'If we both get in, then we've got years of studying ahead of us.'

'Yes, but you'll be in Scotland or London…'

'There *are* trains, Rachel.'

And now, all these years later, sitting on a changing room bench with her head in her hands, Rachel could still recall with absolute precision the glowing feeling those words had delivered.

Who *was* that woman? Rachel thought as

she recalled the ecstasy and unbridled passion that had once been the norm between them.

Who was that woman who had shed her clothes with ease, who had physically ached to be with another person?

Where had she gone?

'There you are,' May said as she peered into the changing room and saw Rachel sitting there, with her head still in her hands.

'Sorry,' Rachel said. 'I was just…' *Just what?* 'Getting my cardigan.'

'It's fine.' May smiled. 'I'm just about to go for my break—why don't you do the same?'

'Sounds great.'

They walked to the staff room together. 'Now, take a seat and I'll get us both a cuppa,' May said.

But there was to be no solace in the staff room for Rachel, because Dominic was sitting there—and not by chance.

Richard had made it very clear that he wanted this dealt with quickly, and so Dominic had sat waiting.

Wondering.

Wondering about Rachel Walker, who, for

the shortest of whiles, had once been Rachel Hadley.

'Tea?' he heard May say as they came in to the staff room.

'I'll have coffee,' Rachel said, and then hurriedly added, 'But I'll get it.'

She did a quick about-turn when she saw Dominic, and May, who he knew liked to make a fuss of her staff when she could, halted her.

'Don't be daft,' May said. 'How do you have it?'

White with one sugar, Dominic was tempted to answer.

'White, no sugar,' Rachel said.

So she had given up that pleasure.

May turned to Dominic. 'How's young Thomas doing?'

'Stable,' Dominic said. 'Which is a hell of a lot better than he was a couple of hours ago.'

'Indeed,' May agreed. 'Would you like some tea?'

'Aye,' he answered in a thick northern accent. 'But none of that namby-pamby herbal stuff...'

May gave a slightly bemused smile, because of course she didn't get the private joke that had once existed between them: Rachel had been in a camomile tea phase, and Dominic, who had been strictly a coffee drinker, had unwittingly made camomile tea for her dad when he'd dropped by their flat.

'What the bloody hell is this?' Dave Walker had said as he'd spat it out.

Yes, he'd thought Dominic a pansy who drank *namby-pamby* herbal tea.

Dominic looked over at Rachel, to see if they might share a private smile, but she was staring hard at the television on the wall and continued to stare at it even as May headed to the kitchen and they were left alone.

'Aren't you going to say hello, Rachel?' Dominic asked.

'Hello.'

Rachel turned and looked at him, but couldn't help her eyes drifting from his dark eyes to his jaw, to his mouth.

His mouth had always enthralled her.

The mouth that had kissed every inch of her skin.

'How have you been?' she asked.

But it was clear Dominic wasn't going to answer that here.

'Do you want to meet for a drink? Clear the air and catch up?'

'No, thanks.' She shook her head, but then, worrying that she'd appear petty, and knowing they had to have this conversation at some point if they were going to be able to work in the same hospital, she changed her mind. 'Actually, a quick catch-up might be good.'

'There's a pub across the road from the hospital,' Dominic suggested. 'I should finish around six—'

'My lunch is at one,' Rachel interrupted. 'If you want to speak we can meet then.'

'I am *not* doing this in the canteen.'

And neither would she be going to a pub with him.

Those days were long since gone.

'It's not as if we're going to be holding hands across the table, Dominic,' Rachel said, but then she questioned her own wisdom. After all, she wanted this kept well away from work.

But Dominic was already nodding.

'I'll do my best to be there,' he replied, rather tartly.

They fell into silence as May came in with a tray of drinks and a huge coffee-and-walnut cake which she had brought from home. Dominic fell upon it immediately, and devoured his slice in a few bites.

He'd always been hungry, Rachel recalled.

'Will you have a piece, Rachel?' May offered.

'Not for me, thanks.' She was struggling to hold her mug of coffee, let alone negotiate eating cake.

'Oh, while I've got you, Dominic…' May chatted on as she cut the cake. 'The Emergency Department are having a night out for all those who worked at Christmas and couldn't make the do.'

'That would be me,' Dominic said.

'So, shall I put you down?' May asked as she handed him a second generous slice. 'We haven't finalised where just yet.'

'I'm not sure…' Dominic said, and then glanced over to Rachel, who was back to staring at the television screen. 'I'll check my roster and let you know.'

'You've already put your name down, haven't you, Rachel?' May said, taking out a list from her pocket and reading through it. 'That's right—Rachel, plus one.' May smiled. 'It will be lovely to meet your fiancé. What's his name again?'

The air seemed to have been sucked out of the room. 'Gordon,' Rachel said rather flatly.

'That's right—Gordon.' May nodded, but then frowned as Dominic abruptly stood up. 'Where are you going in such a hurry? Don't you want that second piece of cake?'

'I've got to see that COPD patient.' He clipped out the words as he stalked off.

Rachel fought not to turn her head at his rapid departure and continued to stare at the television screen.

Oh, dear...oh, dear...oh, dear...

CHAPTER THREE

IN AN EFFORT to save money for the wedding, Rachel had brought her own packed lunch to work. Sitting in the canteen, she peeled the lid off her sandwich box and stared at the slice of frittata that Gordon had made. They'd spent Sunday cooking at home, preparing for the week ahead, with Rachel telling herself that she'd soon get the swing of this new domesticity and that it was exactly what she wanted.

Her mind crept back to long-ago Sundays, lazy café breakfasts and making love in the afternoon…

The frittata didn't appeal, but perhaps that was because she was too nervous about speaking with Dominic to feel hungry. She regretted suggesting the canteen, but a cosy catch-up in the pub had felt too hard at the time. This way they'd just look like two hospital workers sitting at the same table.

That was all they were now.

She scanned the canteen and saw Dominic lining up to pay for his lunch. She put on her best poker face as he made his way over.

'Rachel,' Dominic said as he approached the table.

How odd, she thought, to hear her name from his lips. 'Dominic,' she responded politely and attempted a smile, but her mouth flat-lined like an asystole cardiac arrest and there was nothing she could do to revive it.

The huge roast beef baguette, the slice of cheesecake and mug of coffee on the tray that he plonked down on the table in front of him indicated that the prospect of lunch with his ex-wife hadn't interfered with *his* appetite.

As if to further cement that fact, he took from his pocket a bar of chocolate and put that down on the table too.

'Hungry?' Rachel commented.

'Always.' He nodded and glanced at her sandwich box. 'What are you having?'

It was easier to speak about their food than their past. 'Frittata.'

'Quiche without the best bit?' Dominic

said, and briefly screwed up his nose at her choice of lunch. 'So, what brings you to The Primary?'

'I could ask the same of you,' Rachel said. 'I had no idea you wanted to be a doctor…'

'Well, you wouldn't have,' Dominic clipped. 'It's not as if you kept in touch.'

'Neither did you.'

She took a swift gulp of water to dilute the surge of venom that threatened to lace her voice, because it still galled, still burnt, still hurt that he had left without so much as a backward glance.

'So, how have you been?'

'I can't complain.' He put down the baguette he had started eating. 'Look, this is awkward, I know…'

'I don't feel awkward,' Rachel refuted. 'I'm just taken aback to find you working here.'

'Same.' He nodded. 'Especially as you always said you'd never leave Sheffield.'

Location had been a bone of contention between them. A born-and-bred Yorkshire girl, she had said she never wanted to leave, whereas Dominic had never wanted to be there in the first place.

'I was eighteen when I said that,' she pointed out coldly.

'True,' he conceded, then took another bite of his baguette.

Rachel sneaked a closer look. His hair was more tousled than this morning, and he looked more like the Dominic she'd once known. He was different in other ways, though. She noticed the little fan of lines beside his eyes, and there was already a shadow to his jaw when there hadn't been one this morning. The Dominic she had married had only shaved once a week. She noticed, too, the arrogant edge to him that hadn't been there before.

'We all say stupid things when we're young,' Rachel added.

'We do,' Dominic agreed, and their eyes properly met and held for the very first time since their unexpected reunion. 'You didn't answer my question, Rachel,' Dominic said, still holding her gaze. 'What brings you here?'

It was Rachel who flicked her eyes away. 'My fiancé got a transfer and…well, nursing's pretty portable.'

'So when's the wedding?'

'We haven't set a date yet,' Rachel said.

'You're living together?' he asked, then retracted his question. 'Sorry, that's none of my business.'

'Yes,' she said—because, yes, it was none of his business, but also, yes, she and Gordon were living together. Well, they had been for all of ten days…

'How long have you been together?'

'Nearly three years now.'

'Oh.'

He looked as if he were about to say something else, but then changed his mind and took a huge bite of his baguette instead. He chewed carefully and then swallowed, but it must have stuck a little in his throat because he took a slug of his drink and then offered a comment.

'You're not exactly rushing into things, then?'

'I did that once,' Rachel responded tartly, and saw a small flicker of a smile on his mouth.

His mouth.

Yes, that one.

And this time she could not haul her thoughts away. They had taken each other to bliss over and over and over and, although it scared her to admit it even to herself, she had never quite found that bliss again.

'How's the family?' Dominic asked.

'Much the same.' Rachel nodded. 'Well, bigger. There are a lot of nieces and nephews. How's yours?' she asked.

'I don't see an awful lot of them. I haven't really since…' He swallowed. 'Well, they didn't exactly help matters.'

They had cut him off at the knees when Dominic had married her. They hadn't even sent a card, let alone attended the wedding. She looked up at the man who had, despite his family's strong objections, once stood by her.

'They're back living in London,' he said, 'but we just catch up at Christmas…things like that.'

'I'm sorry you fell out because of us.'

He smiled grimly. 'Don't take all the credit—it honestly wasn't down to you.'

'I ought to get back soon,' Rachel said, packing up her sandwich box.

'But we haven't caught up.'

'What is there to say, Dominic?' She gave a helpless shrug. 'What do you want to know?'

'Are you happy?'

He asked as if it mattered. And she answered as if she were certain.

'Yes.'

Except she hadn't really paused to examine it of late. Her relationship with Gordon had progressed much more slowly than the hurtling freight train of her and Dominic.

Of course she was happy, Rachel told herself.

Okay, maybe she wasn't as deliriously happy as she had been in the early days with Dominic, but she'd been a teenager back then, and flooded with a cocktail of hormones which had ensured she'd felt everything so much more acutely.

His dark brown eyes were frowning slightly as he waited for her to elaborate on her state of happiness.

'I'm very happy,' she said finally. 'Gordon and I both want the same things.'

'What things?' Dominic asked.

'You know…a house, a family…' Rachel's

voice trailed off. She was scared to ask herself if that was *all* that she wanted. 'And you?' she asked. 'Are you happy?'

'Yep,' Dominic said, but did not elaborate.

'You asked for this catch-up, Dominic,' she pointed out, because he wasn't exactly helping the conversation. 'What is it you want to talk about?'

'Okay, I'll ask. Is it going to be a problem for you—us working together?'

'Of course not.' She smiled, but he did not return it. 'Is it a problem for you?'

'Yes.'

She was taken aback by his directness. 'Are you saying you want me to resign…?'

'For God's sake!' he snapped.

It was something she'd never seen him do before. She was starting to realise that Dominic was an entirely different beast now.

'I'm not asking you to resign. I'm just trying to have an honest conversation, Rachel—but then, you were never very good at that.'

'Meaning?' Her hackles were rising—not that she let them show. 'I never lied to you, Dominic.'

'You never told the truth, though. I practically had to be a mind-reader to work out what you were thinking.' He took in a breath—a long one—and gave it to her straight. 'Yes, it's a problem having my ex-wife working at the same hospital as me.'

Oh!

'And I don't know how you're going to react when…' He didn't finish.

It looked as if Dominic wasn't sure quite how to discuss his love life with Rachel.

Or rather, his sex life.

'Are you seeing anyone?' Rachel forced herself to ask. 'Because if it's going to be an issue for her, then I can assure you—'

'Them,' Dominic said, and took another bite of his baguette.

'Them?' Rachel frowned.

'What I mean is, I'm not seeing anyone seriously enough to bring an ex-wife into the equation.'

'I see,' Rachel said, even though she didn't. She couldn't imagine him playing the field.

'I have no intention of getting involved with anyone or making any kind of commitment. I'm not very good at relationships,'

Dominic said, and gave her a slightly twisted smile. 'Though I don't have to tell *you* that.'

'I'm not so sure,' Rachel said. 'We had...'

She blew out a breath and tried to haul her mind back from the place it was dancing towards: the good times, the great times, the best of times.

'It wasn't all bad.'

'It wasn't all *good*.'

And therein lay the difference between them.

If she laid together the years of her life on a grid, then seventeen and eighteen would be tall towers that dwarfed the rest. Those two years with Dominic had been the utter highs.

Yes, their future had sunk, and the bills had piled high, but when the light had been switched off, the door closed on the day, and it had been them...*just them*...

'I don't know how I feel about seeing you again,' Dominic admitted. 'I would really like to shrug...to say, *It's good to see you happy, Rachel*. But I wouldn't be telling the truth.'

'Oh...'

'I'm not going to lie and pretend I'm okay with this.'

'I really don't see the issue,' Rachel said. 'It was years ago. We're different people now—well, you certainly are.'

'Yes,' he said. 'I am.'

Dominic had had to reinvent himself after their failed marriage.

Freshers' Week? What a joke. He had looked around at the sea of happy faces, all excited to start the next phase of their lives, and all he had felt was wrung out.

Everyone had been introducing themselves, getting to know each other. Would anyone want to hear that he was separated, with a divorce pending? That he was a father without a son and looking for a job in order to finish paying for the funeral.

Ask about my gap year? Please don't.

He hadn't wanted to wade through that hellish time with strangers. He hadn't wanted to get close to anyone when the one person he had wanted to get close to had completely shut him out.

But instead of being entirely antisocial,

as he'd wished to, he'd fallen into bar work to support himself and discovered the art of meaningless conversation—and, even better, meaningless sex.

Apart from one maudlin night, when Dominic had lapsed and admitted the truth to Jordan and his wife, Heather, he'd let no one in—because there was nothing he wanted them to see.

After a scare with another woman, despite being hyper-vigilant about birth control, Dominic had gone and got the snip to ensure it could never happen again—and he *revelled* in his infertility.

As his ex-wife was probably about to find out.

No, he did not want her here.

'I could lie,' he said suddenly, and flashed a smile and his white even teeth. 'If that's what you want me to do. Rachel, *hello*! It's *brilliant* to see you!' he exclaimed, and he knew there wasn't even a trace of sarcasm to his tone—except he'd just told her that he didn't mean a word of it. 'Gordon seems *so* good for you.'

She rolled her eyes.

'It's *so* nice to catch up!' Dominic persisted with his taunt. 'I've been *dying* to know what happened to you—'

'Stop it!' she snapped, and for the first time she let him glimpse that, despite her cool façade, she was struggling too. 'You don't have to outright lie,' Rachel said. 'But at the very least I'm sure we can manage to be professional and polite.'

'*That* I can do.'

'Good.'

'But it goes both ways,' Dominic warned her. 'I mean it, Rachel. I expect the same from you.'

'You'll get it. I would never let my past interfere with my work.'

Only perhaps she didn't understand what he was saying—so Dominic made it clear. 'Please don't think that just because we were married for five minutes it gives you any licence to lecture me.'

'Why would I lecture you?'

'Maybe not lecture...' Dominic said. 'But I date, Rachel. I date a *lot*.'

'That's fine. It's none of my business.'

'Exactly.'

* * *

Except Rachel felt her nostrils tighten and pinch, for she loathed the thought of him with someone else. Lots of someone elses.

She hated herself for it, but couldn't help asking, 'When you say *a lot*...?'

'I'm single,' Dominic said, 'and I'm staying that way. But that doesn't mean I've taken a vow of celibacy.'

'That's your choice.'

'Yes, it is,' Dominic said, 'and one that I'll continue to make even if my ex-wife is working in the same building.'

'About that...' Rachel said. 'I think it would be better if we don't tell anyone we were married.' She registered his quick swallow. 'You haven't told anyone, surely?'

'I said something to Richard—my boss. I didn't say that it was you...just that I'd run into my ex-wife.'

'Why would you do that?'

He answered with a question of his own. 'Will you tell your fiancé that your ex-husband is working at The Primary?' Dominic asked.

She glanced up, a little stunned by the question. 'That's different…'

'Not really,' Dominic said. 'Aside from the fact we work together all day, Richard's a good friend. He knew something was up and he asked.'

Rachel let out a breath.

'So?' Dominic persisted. 'Will you tell your fiancé?'

'Yes,' Rachel said, though she wasn't so sure.

There was a knot in her chest—a whole matted knot of emotions that she wasn't sure she wanted to dissect. Of course the answer should be yes. After all, she and Gordon didn't keep secrets. He knew about her past.

'Rachel, there is one other thing I'd like to say.' Dominic interrupted her thoughts. 'And not just because we're going to be working together. It's something I've wanted to be able to say to you for a long time…'

He shifted in his seat and then those velvet brown eyes met hers.

He took a breath and looked right at her. 'I'm sorry that I wasn't able to adequately support you.'

She frowned, and then gave a sort of half-laugh. 'We were eighteen, Dominic. We got by. Well, barely… But—'

'I'm not talking about financially. I know I didn't handle things as well as I could have when you lost the baby…'

It had been her dad who'd alerted Rachel to the fact that her period was late. Not through conversation—they were far too awkward to talk about that type of thing. She'd taken a break from her studies to make lunch for her dad when he'd come back from doing the weekly shop. And there on the bench was a bag just for her, containing her 'bits'—pink deodorant and pink razors, tampons and pads. Enough for an entire pack of Girl Guides, because her dad got embarrassed buying them so got a job lot every couple of months.

And it was then she'd realised that she was late.

A few days of silent panic later she had taken a test and then curled up on her bed and wished, more than ever, that her mum was alive—for she would surely have known what to do.

Her exams had been awful. Everything Rachel knew, everything she had learnt, had flown out of the window as she'd panicked at the prospect of telling her dad.

And Dominic.

She'd waited outside the school, where he'd been sitting a physics exam, and he'd come out wearing a wide relieved smile—which had soon faded when she'd shared her news.

'I've got a doctor's appointment this afternoon,' Rachel had added, when Dominic had said nothing.

'So it's not definite, then?'

'The test says I am.'

'But we're *always* careful.'

And they had been. They'd used condoms every single time. But a dull flush had come to her cheeks as they'd walked.

One time.

One time they'd dozed and then started fooling around again. When he'd entered her for a second time, they'd lingered a while before putting the condom on.

But that had been ages ago.

Months…

'I think my dad's guessed,' she'd admitted as they walked through the park. 'I keep on being sick. I told him it was just exam nerves, but now the exams are over…'

'Why didn't you tell me when you first found out?' he'd demanded.

'Because I wanted at least one of us to pass the exams!'

Rachel had wanted to hide it for as long as possible, but Dominic had faced it head-on.

His parents had been appalling, and had made it clear what a disappointment their son was, and later they had even told Rachel that she was bringing their son down to her working-class level.

Her father's reaction…

Well, Rachel would never know what his initial reaction had been.

Dominic had insisted *he* would deal with it, so she had sat in a bar, nursing a grapefruit juice, while he had spoken to her father alone.

'Was he angry?' she'd asked when Dominic had joined her.

'More worried than angry,' Dominic had said. 'He asked what I intended to do about it. I told him that I'll take care of you both… that we'll get married.'

'Married?' She'd shaken her head. Because in her most private thoughts, before the pregnancy, she'd dreamt of that.

Just not like this.

Never like this.

'Your dad's offered me a job.'

'But you're going to university. That's what you've always wanted.'

'Rachel, we're having a *baby*!'

That was when, for the first time, it had started to sink in. They had sat there, staring at each other, both a little stunned as reality hit.

'I'm going to defer,' Dominic had told her. 'Assuming I get the right results…'

'You'll get them.'

'I'll work my backside off this year,' Dominic had gone on. 'And maybe next year, once the baby's here…' His voice had trailed off, but then he'd rallied. 'We'll get there.'

A month later they'd been married at Sheffield Town Hall. Her family had been there to cheer them on, dressed in suits and wearing wide smiles, whereas his family had refused to attend and hadn't sent so much as a card.

His family, who would have happily supported him through his degree, had cut Dominic off at the knees in an attempt to force him away from Rachel.

Her dad had offered them a place to live for a while—at home with him. But Dominic had refused.

'I can't live *and* work with him, Rachel.'

'Meaning…?' She had been instantly defensive, but Dominic had refused to elaborate.

After a little celebration in her dad's back garden they had headed for the tiny flat they had rented.

For the first couple of months of their marriage it had felt a little like a game. Back then, as they'd realised they were a married couple—a *real* married couple—they'd enjoyed the freedom and privacy of having their own place, with no parents to check on them or tell them to leave the bedroom door open.

'You can do your exams again,' Dominic had told her when the results had come in.

Dominic had aced his, yet he'd deferred his studies, as he'd promised, and taken the job with her father and her brothers.

'Just till we get sorted,' he'd said.

But they had never got themselves sorted, no matter how hard they'd tried.

And now here they were, face to face in a hospital canteen, looking back on their lives, with Dominic trying to speak to her about the most difficult part: their baby.

'I really don't want to discuss it here, Dominic.' She snapped the top down on her little sandwich box and screwed the lid on her water bottle.

'You're the one who suggested the canteen.'

'Yes—and now I have to get back.'

They were all caught up. What more was there to say that could be said in a place like this? That she would ever want to say?

'But you haven't eaten your frittata.'

That made her smile.

'It's no fun without the pastry.'

It was a tiny joke, yet it smacked of *them*, of how they'd used to be, of how easy it had once been between them. And when he gave a low laugh her regret was instant.

She'd missed that laugh.

She'd missed him.

Missed *them*.

Oh, Houston, Rachel thought, *we have a problem!*

Rachel let herself into her flat and with a sigh of relief closed the door on a wretched day.

Gordon had texted to say he'd be late and it had come as a relief.

Should she tell him that Dominic was working at The Primary?

Of course she should.

It was no big deal.

She took off her coat and kicked off her shoes, but instead of putting them away, instead of flicking on the kettle or turning her mind to dinner, she padded through to the bedroom and closed the curtains. Half an hour of sleep might get rid of the headache that had been building all day.

Or rather, the heartache. The ache of the scar tissue wrapped around a heart that had had to learn to beat again.

She had deeply mourned both the end of her marriage and the death of their son, and for a long time her grief had felt insurmountable.

And now, on this particular evening, Rachel stared at the wall and watched her own private screening of the best and worst times in her life.

There she was at the start of their short marriage, standing on the gorgeous staircase in Sheffield Town Hall, so happy to be Dominic's wife.

So very, incredibly happy.

She'd worn an ochre dress, and there had been just the hint of her bump, but it was her smile that stood out, and it had been captured in a photo.

But then she'd turned to her new husband and seen his smile, and she had known he was faking it—or at the very least not as delirious with joy as she was on their wedding day.

Of course they'd made love on their wedding night. After all, they were very good at that. But despite the ring on her finger, despite the baby inside her and despite the passion between them, for Rachel there had been something missing.

She'd waited for those words as she'd lain there in the dark, needing to be told by her husband that he loved her.

Those words had never come.

It hadn't been her imagination, and it hadn't been her making a big deal of things. She'd known that Dominic didn't love her the way she loved him.

But love would grow, she had told herself.

Once the baby had arrived, once they'd got on top of things, his feelings would deepen and change.

And so, knowing that he didn't quite love her, Rachel had chosen not to tell him that she loved *him*.

Ever so, *ever so* much.

As their school pals had all headed off to university, or for a gap year trekking in Nepal or building houses in Africa, Dominic had taken the job in her father's removals business and together the two of them had attempted to make a home in a flat above a shop.

Rachel had got a job in a hairdresser's,

washing hair, sweeping, tidying and making drinks, and Dominic had taken an extra job in a local bar in the evenings.

They had lived for a while in that little idyll, working hard, saving hard for the baby.

And, as Dominic had often said, sex didn't cost a thing…

Until one sleepy morning, a couple of weeks before her due date, his hand had come to rest on her stomach, waiting for a little kick before he headed to work.

Waiting…

'He's still asleep,' Dominic had said.

They'd already found out they were having a boy.

'Did he kick last night?' Rachel had turned and rolled onto her back. 'Dominic, I can't remember if he kicked.'

'Of course he did,' Dominic had soothed.

She'd moved her hand to her stomach and pushed her fingers down…waiting.

Waiting…

Forever waiting…

The labour had been horrific.

Even now, thirteen years on, Rachel was unable to relive it. So she pressed fast forward on that part—and fast forward on the funeral as well—to the time they had gone back to their little flat.

Except they hadn't known how to *be* with each other—how to touch, how to sit, how to sleep, how to speak after all that.

To be fair, Dominic had tried.

'If you want me to stay home I can ask your dad if I can take a few more days,' he had said, when his alarm clock had gone off two weeks after their loss.

A few more days?

The little Moses basket had been returned, as well as all the baby clothes, and the bags of nappies had been donated, but she'd kept a little pair of socks.

Her dad had paid for the funeral, but Dominic had insisted it was a loan. He'd loathed—*loathed*—the fact that he hadn't had the money to bury his son, and he wanted to work to pay every penny of it back.

'Go to work,' she'd mumbled, and turned away from him.

Go to work so I can close my eyes on this nightmare, she'd been thinking.

But Dominic had wanted to talk.

'A book I was reading last night says that you'll want to speak about him…that we should talk about the baby—'

'His name's Christopher!' she'd snapped, and looked into bemused brown eyes that were looking at her as if she were a stranger.

'Talk to me,' Dominic had said. 'Tell me how you're feeling.'

As if everyone I love leaves. My mum. My baby. And soon you will leave me too, and I can't bear it. I cannot bear the thought of it all being over. I know you were only with me because of the baby. Christopher. If he'd lived… But I can't go there, because he didn't. I lost our baby and now I'm going to lose you. I'm losing you already, and we both know it…

She'd felt as if her grief were too big to traverse, and she had not known how to share her pain nor voice her fears. She'd been told so many times that her tears and her drama only made things worse.

'Go to work,' she'd said again, and rolled away from him.

And so life had hurtled on, when she'd

wished it might stop for a while and let her grieve for her terrible loss.

'Come on now, lass,' her dad had said when he'd come to visit them in their little flat and Rachel hadn't been able to face getting out of bed. 'I know it's difficult, but lying in bed and mooching around the flat is getting you nowhere. When your mum died I had to get back to work, and to tell the truth, it helped.'

Instead of sympathy cards thudding through the door, it had soon been bills, and even Dominic, with his mathematical brain, had struggled to make sense of them.

Water bills.

Gas bills.

Final reminder notices.

At the six-week follow-up appointment with her obstetrician, Rachel had been told there was nothing she could have done differently to change the outcome.

'Can we try again?' she had asked the doctor, because her arms had ached for her baby. Ached to hold her tiny boy, with his little pinched face and slender hands.

She'd turned when she'd heard Dominic's sharp intake of breath and had seen his eyes shutter in his shell-shocked face as the doctor had told them that while there was nothing to suggest it would happen again, she would be monitored very closely next time.

They had walked past the other mothers at their postnatal check-ups, with their carry slings and prams and the *wah-wah-wah* noise of newborns crying, and Rachel and Dominic had each been in separate versions of silence.

Rachel, bereft.

Dominic, stunned.

It had been Dominic who had broken the silence as they'd walked through the park. 'What did you mean, try again?'

She hadn't been able to answer, so Dominic had answered for her.

'Rachel, we are *not* trying for another baby. I'm going to university next year.'

She had heard the determination in his voice, as if there was no other option to consider.

He was already thinking of the future.

One she didn't want to see.

'In London?' she asked.

'Yes,' Dominic said calmly.

'We can't afford London—we're barely getting by here.'

'I've already got a place.'

'So I've got to follow you wherever you go?'

'Not if you don't want to,' Dominic had said. Then, 'Jesus, Rachel, that pregnancy just about finished you, and seeing you—' Dominic had halted. 'Seeing him…' His lips had turned white and he'd swallowed hard.

It had incensed her that he still couldn't bring himself to say their son's name. 'His name's *Christopher*!'

'I know his name, Rachel!'

For the first time ever Dominic had shouted, but then he'd reined it in and taken her cold hands in his.

'I know I should have taken better care… I should never have got you pregnant. Look, I've done everything I can to make it right, but…' He'd shaken his head. 'I'm never putting you through that again. I'm never putting *myself* through that again. There isn't going to be another baby.' He'd paused and shaken his head again. *'Ever.'*

Back at their little flat, Rachel had gone to

bed. Lying on her side in the darkened room, she'd pretended to be asleep when he'd come to check on her. And there she had lain, hearing the doorbell and then the arrival—for the first time—of his parents at their flat, as well as the conversation that had ensued.

'You can put all this behind you,' Professor Hadley had said.

'Can you please keep your voice down?' Dominic had asked. 'Rachel's asleep.'

'Is she *still* not working?'

'She's just lost a baby!'

There had been more muffled words and then his dad's voice had cut through the gloom.

'You used to have a future. As far as I can see, the only thing she's doing is bringing you down. It's time to put this mess behind you and pick up your life where you left off.'

As harsh as Professor Hadley's words were, it had been nothing Rachel hadn't been thinking herself. Dominic seemed fine, while her whole world had crumbled.

They'd limped on for a couple more months, until finally Dominic had sat down on the edge of the bed she'd barely got out of in those days.

'Listen,' he'd said, and taken her hand. 'What if I ask your dad if we can move in with him for a few months? I can work like crazy and we can get ahead—and you can take some time and focus on retaking your exams.'

She'd looked up at him, up to the dark of his eyes, and then down to the mouth that had never once said the words she'd needed to hear.

'Or *I* could move in with my dad.'

'What are you talking about?'

'Dominic, why did you marry me?'

'Rachel—'

'Why?'

The silence was endless. 'What do you want me to say here, Rachel? I'm trying to do the best I can.'

'But why did you marry me?'

'Because you were pregnant—because it was the right thing to do...'

She'd known all along that Dominic had only married her because of the baby. And now that there wasn't one...

Rachel had removed her hand from his and then she had removed herself from his life.

Mourning both her marriage and her baby had been a mountain it had taken years to climb. Her long-time dream of being a midwife had evaporated, and she'd simply not known who she was any more.

She'd moved back to her dad's, returned to work at the hairdresser's—this time as an apprentice.

There she'd made friends, and later she'd moved out of her dad's. She had finally rediscovered what it meant to have dreams, to want something in the future. But she no longer wanted to be a midwife, so she had applied to study nursing and had fallen in love with Emergency.

It had taken years, but piece by piece she had built a new life.

A good life.

A nice life.

And yet it didn't hold a candle to the bliss she had once known.

The good times with Dominic had been the very best of times, Rachel thought now, as she lay there, recalling the utter joy of lying in his arms, the sheer heady pleasure of their lovemaking. But it hadn't all been sex.

She had never been happier than when they'd scored a lunch break together and would sit in a café or bar, holding hands. Or when they sat at their little kitchen table and he tested her for when she'd retake her exams. When she'd cut his hair. When they'd stood in their little living room, Dominic tall, her massive with her baby bump, and danced and laughed and danced…

She'd never been so happy in all her life.

And later, as she scraped the remains of her lunch from the sandwich box into the little compost bin that they kept under the sink, Rachel herself loathed the analogy, even if it smacked of the truth:

She and Gordon were frittata.

CHAPTER FOUR

BREAKING UP REALLY was hard.

Perhaps more so when you were the one taking an axe to a perfectly good relationship with a nice and kind man.

Had she not bumped into Dominic…

Rachel truly didn't know what would have happened.

But by the end of the week, when she still hadn't told her fiancé that her ex-husband was working at The Primary, Rachel accepted the reason why.

She should have been able to tell Gordon, reassuring him that it wasn't a problem, that Dominic meant nothing.

Nothing.

She should have been able to say airily, *Oh, that was years ago...* And, *If Dominic was the last man on earth I wouldn't...*

Except, Dominic had been the *first.*

She certainly wasn't breaking up with Gordon in the hope of rekindling things with her ex. It was more that she could not bear the thought of putting Gordon through what she had experienced.

He deserved love.

'Is there someone else?' Gordon hurled the inevitable question at her.

A week ago she would have been able to look him in the eye and say, *No, of course not. Absolutely not.*

Except…

'Rachel?' Gordon demanded.

She truly didn't know how to answer him, for it had hit her then: there had always been someone else taking up too much space in both her mind and her heart.

Dominic Hadley.

Yes, breaking up really was hard to do.

There was a lot of slamming things in suitcases—Gordon.

And a whole lot of silence—Rachel.

She really was still terrible at sharing her feelings.

When the door slammed closed she sat there, in silence rather than in tears, and wondered if she should research if there were any adult education classes she could take in How to Share Your Feelings.

She felt…*defeated.*

It was the best word she could come up with.

Defeated because she had worked so very hard for so many years and tried so very hard to move on.

She had tried to let love into her life. She had moved her world to be with Gordon. But here she was, alone, her world turned upside down…again.

There was never a more honest hour than the one just after a relationship died.

Rachel wanted a family, and she wanted a baby, and while she'd been content with Gordon, she hadn't been as happy as she'd told Dominic she was.

She hadn't loved Gordon. At least not in the white-hot way she had loved Dominic—not that she'd ever dared to reveal it to him. She had always been so good at keeping her feelings under wraps.

But Dominic hadn't loved her.

And she must never forget that fact.

* * *

When she had a couple of days off on the rota, Rachel took the train up to Sheffield to tell her dad that her engagement to Gordon was off.

She wanted to tell him in private, without a running commentary and input from her brothers, but it took some considerable time to find a moment alone with him. The doorbell or the phone were constantly ringing, with one of her brothers or their wives, or one of her ten nieces and nephews, all of whom Rachel adored.

Except today. Especially today. It felt as if she was always the aunt and never the mum, and destined to remain that way for ever.

As if to ram home that fact, Phil and his wife dropped by with the happy news that Rachel would soon be an aunt for the eleventh time. She had never been more grateful for the ability to hide her true feelings.

But finally she stood in the kitchen alone with her dad.

'So, how are you finding the new job?' he asked as he stacked the dishwasher while Rachel made them a cup of tea.

'I like it,' Rachel admitted. 'The hospital's really busy, but the staff are nice. There's a big work do coming up and I've put my name down to go…' Her voice trailed off, and it took her a moment to find it again. 'Dad, I've got something to tell you. I broke up with Gordon.'

She watched as her dad stiffened and then got back to rearranging the mugs on the top rack—the mugs that she herself had put in the dishwasher.

'That was sudden,' her dad said.

'I know.'

'You're okay, though?'

'Dad, it was my choice. I'm honestly fine.'

'Are you going to move back up here?'

'Not yet.' Rachel sighed. 'There's a lease on the flat and…' She shrugged. 'I think I like London.'

'Really?'

'I didn't just move there because of Gordon.'

She'd been ready for change too. But she hadn't foreseen this much change.

She was single again, and in a new city, with a new job and no friends nearby to call on…and her ex-husband working at the same hospital. Not that she would be getting into a deep and meaningful conversation about *that* with her dad.

'I'm sure the right one's out there for you,' her dad said, doing his best to offer relationship advice to his daughter. 'Better to find out now than later.'

Was it?

Rachel wasn't so sure.

How could it possibly be better to find out all these years on, just as you were finally moving on with your life, with an upcoming marriage and the possibility of babies on the horizon, that you weren't as over your ex as you'd hoped?

Of course she didn't say that to her dad, though he had something of his own to add. 'While we're on the subject of romance and such,' her dad said, 'I've got a lady friend coming to dinner tonight.'

'What?' Rachel frowned, because in the twenty-six years since her mother had died there had never been so much as a hint of anyone else. 'Are you saying you're seeing someone? How long has this been going on?' Rachel asked. 'Is it serious? Are you—?'

'Moira,' he said. 'Her name's Moira.'

And that was all Dave Walker had to say on the subject of his love life. Though when Moira arrived he had plenty to say about Rachel's.

Moira, Rachel guessed, was younger than her dad—in her early sixties, perhaps, with straight white hair cut in a rather stunning jagged bob which, given Rachel's brief hairdressing career, she noticed and admired. Beyond the bob, she considered that, since Moira's hair was a beautiful white, rather than grey, she had very possibly been a redhead.

Like Rachel's mum.

And that was more than enough to make Rachel wary.

'It's lovely to meet you, Rachel.' Moira smiled. 'I was sorry we didn't get a chance to meet before you headed down to London.'

'Moira had other plans on the day of your leaving party,' her dad explained.

'No, I didn't, Dave,' Moira said, and Rachel

couldn't help but smile. 'You just thought it a bit soon for the kids to be told.'

'Well, you're here now,' Dave huffed. 'Come on through.'

He guided them to the dining room, where they sat down at the table—usually they ate in the kitchen or in the lounge. He handed Moira a glass of wine and soon brought up the reason for Rachel's unexpected visit. 'Rachel's just broken off her engagement.'

'Oh, that can't have been an easy decision,' Moira said. 'Or was it?'

Rachel certainly wasn't about to reveal anything to a stranger, but before she could find a polite response which would make it clear the subject was not up for discussion, her dad chimed in.

'Probably for the best. Never really took to him myself.'

'You've said that about everyone I've ever been out with.'

'Well, you've brought home some right idiots.'

'Dad, I've hardly brought anyone home.'

'There was that Ricky. The one you worked with when you were hairdressing.'

'Ricky's gay.' Rachel sighed. 'We were just friends. I assume you're referring to Dominic?'

'Hmmph,' Dave said, because he loathed speaking about that time. 'That one couldn't stop a pig in a ginnel.'

He looked at Moira, expecting her to laugh, but halted when Rachel got up from the dining room table and walked out.

He found her in the kitchen staring out at the garden and trying not to cry.

'Come on, lass, I'm just playing. I'm sorry to hear about you and Gordon—but, as I always say, there's no point upsetting yourself.'

But it wasn't Gordon she was upset about.

It was Dominic.

She thought back to the eighteen-year-old Dominic, arriving home after a long day working with her father and brothers before heading out for a shift in a bar that night. He'd asked her what the old Yorkshire saying *couldn't stop a pig in a ginnel* had meant.

'Couldn't stop a pig in an alley,' Rachel had translated. 'It means useless, I guess. Why?'

Dominic had shaken his head rather than say why he was asking. 'It doesn't matter.'

He'd looked so hurt that day, so dejected, but she had never, even for a moment, thought the insult had come from her dad.

She'd spent so long looking back on their time together wearing thorn-rimmed glasses, shaded with the resentment and the pain of what had come after, that she hadn't stopped to think what it had been like for him. And Dominic's apology the other day in the hospital about not providing for her had shaken her. While she knew he hadn't been talking about money, the truth was that Dominic had changed all his plans, worked hard day and night, and tried so hard to take care of both her and the baby.

'Is everything okay?'

Rachel glanced up and saw that Moira was standing at the kitchen door, but she said nothing, safe in the knowledge that her dad would soon shut the conversation down.

Except he didn't!

'She's just a bit upset about the break-up with Gordon.'

'It's not Gordon!' Rachel snapped, and then blurted it out. 'Dominic's working at The Primary.'

'What?' The colour drained out of her father's face.

'He's a doctor there,' Rachel said.

'Who's Dominic?' Moira asked.

Dave gave a weary sigh and ran a worried hand over his scruffy grey beard. 'Our Rachel was married to him for a while,' he said, then added, 'Broke her heart, that fella did.'

'It was a long time ago, Dad,' Rachel said, and tried to rally. 'It's fine. Come on, let's have dinner.'

Dinner was an amazing roast lamb, that Dave had cooked incredibly well, but he was very quiet as Moira kept the conversation careering over to Dominic.

'How long were the two of you married, Rachel?'

'About a year,' Rachel said, and took a large slug of wine. 'Have *you* been married, Moira?'

She was making a point—there were some things you just didn't talk about.

'Twice,' Moira said.

Rachel was glad she'd killed that conversation stone-dead…except it turned out that Moira was just drawing breath.

'First time was wonderful—second time a mistake,' Moira said. 'I swore off men and kept to it for fifteen years. But then your dad and I…'

Rachel closed her eyes and wondered if the talkative Moira was going to tell her that she and her dad had been internet dating—but, no.

'Well, I was downsizing and he came to give me a quote.'

'Oh.'

'I don't know what came over me, but I said, perhaps we could work it out over dinner. Still,' Moira said, 'you don't want to hear about your dad and me. How was it, seeing this Dominic again?'

'Moira…' Dave warned, but Moira took no notice.

'I'm just asking. I dread running into *my* ex.'

'It was fine,' Rachel said airily. 'We had lunch together and caught up.'

'Caught up?' Dave checked. 'On what?'

'Just…' She blew out a breath. 'This and that.'

It was clear her dad didn't like the sound of that and was visibly worried.

'Look, maybe you should just come back home,' he said. 'You're not with Gordon any more—there's nowt to keep you down there.'

But Rachel, who had been thinking the same thing, answered as the woman she wanted to be, rather than the one she was. 'I'm not coming home just because my ex happens to work in the same place. It's a huge hospital. With any luck I'll barely see him.'

With any luck!

CHAPTER FIVE

'HOW WERE YOUR days off?' May asked.

'Great.'

Rachel's response was a little stilted—and not just because Dominic was sitting at the crowded nurses' station. He was writing up some notes after a frantic morning, during which a serious head injury and a cardiac arrest had arrived simultaneously, all on Rachel's first full shift in Resus.

So much for hardly seeing him!

And she felt particularly awkward because she'd told no one about her break-up with Gordon. There was no need to just yet, she'd decided. After all, it wasn't as if she'd ever worn her ring at work. And it just felt somehow safer to say she was in a relationship when she was around Dominic.

Well, not *safer*.

But there was no point muddying things.

'Did you end up going home?' May persisted with the conversation.

'Yes,' Rachel said, and then checked herself, because she was being aloof. It was only Dominic she had to remember to stay entirely professional and polite with—not her colleagues. 'I had dinner with my dad and his new girlfriend.'

'How was it?' May asked.

'Awkward,' Rachel admitted. 'Though she seems nice and everything.'

'Well, I'm sure you'll soon get used to her.' May smiled and then picked up a large envelope and waved it in Dominic's face. 'I need your deposit for the night out. Cash only—I can't be doing with your apps and things. If you change your mind, you won't get it back.' She read down her list to see who else was on it. 'What about you, Jordan?'

'Heather and I will be there.' Jordan nodded. 'I'll have to get the cash to you another day.'

'What about you, Rachel? Oh, you've already paid. What was your man's name again?'

'Gordon!' Dominic answered for her, with

a tart edge that May must have caught because she gave a slow blink.

'So it is!'

'I can't wait,' Tara chimed in, with a smile aimed at Dominic. Rachel felt her nostrils do that pinched thing all over again. 'We're going Greek!'

'Fantastikós,' Dominic said, and took his wallet out and peeled off the necessary notes. 'I'm looking forward to it.'

Indeed Dominic was. Now.

He wanted to be very sure that Rachel Walker didn't think that the fact she'd once been Rachel Hadley gave her any say in how he lived his life.

'Right,' he said, and stood. 'I'm headed up to Maternity before they page me again.'

I've got this, Dominic decided as he made his way.

He and Rachel were all caught up. There was nothing left to say.

There was no way he was going to change his life, or tiptoe around Rachel. They'd spoken, she'd said she was fine with them working in the same building, and she was engaged to someone else. They had both moved on.

But he couldn't deny he was keen to see this Gordon chap for himself.

The man who made Rachel happy.

His skin crawled at the very thought of it, and his jaw was clamped even as he entered the ward.

'Dominic!' Freya, the midwife who was Richard's wife, greeted him warmly as he stepped into the delivery suite. 'We've been waiting for you.'

'I'm sorry it took me so long.' He introduced himself, and apologised to both the patient and her partner for the delay.

'Just don't run off.' The patient, Sonia, gave a weak smile that soon changed into a grimace of agony.

'The last anaesthetist got paged to go to Theatre just as Freya was getting things ready,' explained Josh, Sonia's partner.

'Well, I can vouch for Dominic,' Freya said. 'He gave me *my* epidural and I've been crazy about him ever since.'

It was one of Freya's funny little stories to relax women in labour.

As Dominic set up, he looked over at Josh, who was comforting Sonia and telling her how great she was doing. They were both so young.

Dominic gave a *lot* of epidurals, and usually he could just shut his mind down on the past and get on with the job. But there were days—and this was one of them—when it was impossible to keep the memories away.

'We'll have you feeling a lot more comfortable very soon,' he said as he washed his hands and then put on surgical gloves.

Sonia was amazing. Her partner held her hand and shared a worried glance with Sonia's mother, who was stroking back her hair from her sweaty face. There was just so much love and support in the room.

There was no real comparison to when he and Rachel had gone through this, Dominic told himself. This baby, soon to be born, was healthy and full-term, yet for some reason it was just getting to him, when usually Dominic refused to allow it to do so.

With the epidural secured, he stepped back, and Josh, along with Freya, helped Sonia lie back on the delivery bed.

'You'll be feeling much better soon,' Dominic said.

'I think I'm already starting to.'

'Told you he was good!' Freya said.

Dominic ran through his instructions again, and Freya thanked him as he left, but as he stepped out of the delivery suite, it felt as if the sound of all the babies crying in the unit was playing in stereo in his head.

Wah, wah, wah.

He sat there, trying to write up his notes, as the tiny babies cried and wailed. And all he could think was that he couldn't recall the features of his son with the precision he required.

Dominic didn't have so much as a photo of him.

Rachel had them all.

But it wasn't just her reappearance in his life that had him wanting a photo. He'd tried to get one a few years ago, but the hospital where his son had been born had long since closed down.

Wah, wah, wah.

For Dominic, the worst part was that, despite having been told he had died, despite having seen his still, silent heart on the ultrasound while he was still in Rachel's womb—despite all that—when he'd been born, when Dominic had seen his son for the first time he had still expected him to cry.

Dominic put down his pen and buried his face in his hands, not even noticing that Freya had come to the desk.

'You okay, Dominic?' she checked.

Normally he'd make a joke—especially to a colleague—and laugh it off. But right now he could not make a joke and he could not laugh it off. He was at work on a ward, updating his charts, and about to break down. That would never do.

'Dominic?' Freya checked again.

'I've got a thumping headache.'

He didn't, but for appearances' sake Dominic accepted a glass of water and took a couple of headache pills.

No, he and Rachel were *not* all caught up. They had some unfinished business after all.

He wanted those photos and he was going to ask her for them.

Having made the decision, he headed back down to Emergency. There he found Rachel, restocking the drawers in the Resus nurses' station, and as he tried to decide how best to broach the subject, she shot him a look.

'What?' Dominic said, surprised at the venom in her look when she was normally so inscrutable.

'You know very well what.'

'I don't.'

'You. Earlier,' she said. 'Answering for me.'

'I have no idea what you're talking about.'

'Telling May Gordon's name.'

'So? May forgets names all the time. It was just a little sarcasm aimed at her,' Dominic lied smoothly. 'I was pointing out that even I know your fiancé's name.'

He knew that not for a second did she believe him.

'Don't do it again,' Rachel warned. 'I'm doing my level best to stop this from getting out.'

'Guess what, Rachel?' Dominic answered. 'You don't get to tell me what to do. Don't you remember that conversation we had in the canteen?'

He took a seat and tried to focus on what he'd come here to ask, but Rachel incensed him out of all reasonable proportion with all her no-go zones. Even the scent of her hair as she filled the drawers incensed him—because even all these years on beneath it was the scent of *her*. And it made him speak without thinking.

'I don't see why it has to be such a secret.'

'Don't you?' she checked.

'No. I honestly don't.'

'Perhaps I don't want it to get out that I was married to The Primary Hospital's own resident alley cat.'

'Ha-ha.' He said it sarcastically.

'You've changed,' she accused.

And it wasn't just because he'd become something of a womaniser, thought Rachel. The Dominic she had known had been loyal and faithful. Something twisted inside her as she recalled the slightly shy, somewhat awkward boy she had once known.

But Dominic wasn't apologising for anything these days.

'Of course I've changed,' he retorted. 'From what I recall, the old me wasn't getting very far.' And then he warned her with a pointing of his finger. 'Don't try and police me, Rachel.'

So much for professional and polite!

'I'm just trying to keep the past where it belongs. I've barely been here a week and I do not want to be the topic of gossip.'

She had filled every drawer bar one, and to show him he didn't affect her in the least, she asked him to move—just as she would if it were anyone else—so she could get the last one done.

'Excuse me,' she said.

He shifted his knees to the left without a word, and as her arm brushed his, Rachel wondered if the fire alarms were about to go off, because his very touch scorched.

'Thanks.'

To her displeasure, she knew they were both turned on and trying very hard not to be.

'We clearly need to talk,' Dominic said. 'But away from here.'

'I don't think we do. We've already talked, in the canteen, and said all that needs to be said.'

'There's something I need to ask you and

I'm not comfortable doing it at work. Look, I don't want to make any trouble between you and your fiancé…'

She opened her mouth to tell him that she and Gordon had split up, but closed it as he continued.

'There's that pub I told you about, just across the road from the main entrance,' Dominic said. 'I'm on until six…'

Rachel shook her head. 'I finish at four.'

'Then I'll speak to Richard and see if I can get away early. I'll be there around five and I'd really appreciate it if you would join me.'

And she had to concede, while she did not want to go, that if their paths were going to cross at work, it was going to take more than a ten-minute catch-up in the hospital canteen to work out if it was doable.

Perhaps he'd already decided that it wasn't and he was going to ask her to consider leaving.

And if he did say that they couldn't work together and asked her to go, Rachel pondered as she worked her way through the afternoon, what would her response be?

Righteous indignation and *How dare you*

try and dictate my life thirteen years on? Or would she fold over in sweet relief and say *Yes, of course I'll leave, because I'm finding this impossible too*?

But of course she wouldn't say any of that. Far more likely she would fall back on her usual tactic of not giving him the slightest sign that he was getting to her.

Except he was.

There was a very good reason she didn't want their past getting out. She did not want his name attached to hers. She did not want the inevitable questions and she did not want to have to relive or explain her past when she was struggling to picture a future.

Here.

Working alongside him.

When her shift ended she made her way to the changing rooms, but she still didn't know if she was going to meet Dominic or slink off home. From her locker, Rachel pulled out the jeans, jumper and boots she had worn to work that morning, topped them off with a trench coat, and decided she wouldn't bother with make-up—though usually she'd have put on at least a dash of lipstick if she were catching up with a friend.

Dominic wasn't a friend, though.

May came into the changing room as Rachel was running a brush through her hair before pulling on a woolly hat.

'Any plans for tonight?' May asked.

'Not really,' Rachel said.

She was surprised by how much she wanted to confide in May, to tell her she was thinking of going for a drink with her ex-husband, Dominic, and how conflicted and confused she was feeling about it all. But of course she didn't. The habit was too ingrained. Rachel had long learnt to keep her thoughts to herself.

'Just a quiet one,' she added as she wound a scarf around her neck.

'Well, enjoy.' May smiled and took up her bag and headed out.

Rachel doubted she'd be enjoying herself, but decided that she had to be brave. She would meet with Dominic—just to hear what it was he wanted to ask—and then she'd go home.

He might not have been able to get away

early, Rachel consoled herself as she stepped into the pub.

Except, despite the pub being busy, she saw Dominic straight away.

Gosh, he looked completely amazing as he sat there sulking in a beautiful grey suit. He was drumming his fingers on the table, but when she walked in he looked up immediately and raised his hand in greeting.

Rachel gave him a wave to say that she'd seen him, and then went to the bar to get a drink.

He'd been waiting for fifteen minutes. Richard had agreed that he could leave early to meet Rachel, and had also enquired after his headache. Clearly Dominic was a hot topic of conversation between his boss and his wife. Still, as much as that irked, right now the person who really irked him was Rachel.

He was actually surprised to see her, as he had braced himself for the fact she might not come. Yet here she was, looking utterly gorgeous and quietly, despite his reluctance, turning him on.

She took off her scarf and then her hat, in

a ritual he knew all too well, then shook out her hair—which was lighter than it had been when they were together, and which she wore straight now.

Rachel carried over what he suspected would be grapefruit juice, and placed it on the table before removing her coat.

Dominic had to force himself to remove his gaze, because he did not want to notice her bust in the tight jumper she wore, nor picture the slim pale legs beneath her jeans, or the blaze of gold that lay between them.

'I didn't know if you wanted to eat?' Dominic said. 'I can ask for the menu if you'd like?'

'No, thanks,' Rachel said, and watched as he topped up his sparkling water.

He'd never drunk alcohol—well, only very occasionally—as he always liked to be sharp and had long ago told her he couldn't see the point.

'Was it a problem?' Dominic asked. 'Meeting me tonight?'

She knew he was asking if Gordon knew

she was meeting him, and she didn't know quite what to say, but again she chose not to tell him about the break-up.

'No.' She shook her head. 'It's no problem. So, what is it that you want to ask me?'

'I'll get to that. How are you finding working at The Primary?'

He was questioning her as if he were conducting an interview.

'I like it.' Rachel's response was equally wooden, but then she relaxed and gave him an eye-roll. 'Well, apart from the fact I've just found out that my ex-husband works there.'

'How inconvenient,' Dominic retorted, and they finally shared a smile.

'Very,' she agreed, and then asked, 'How long have you been there?'

'For ever,' Dominic said. 'I did my clinical training there and never left.'

'So when did you decide to become a doctor?' she asked, with what she told herself was curiosity but what she feared was a desperation to know more.

'After you and I broke up I took stock, I

guess, and I had the grades… To tell the truth, I had thought of medicine before, but wasn't sure I'd be any good.'

'But you're the cleverest person I know.'

'I meant socially,' Dominic said. 'But all that time working with your dad taught me a lot.'

'How?'

He shrugged. Clearly he wasn't prepared to open up entirely. 'So, you say he's seeing someone?' he asked.

'Yes.' Rachel nodded.

Dominic was genuinely curious about his former father-in-law.

They hadn't kept in touch, as such. There had been a couple of phone calls that he didn't want to think about, and it had also taken Dominic two years to pay him back for the funeral.

Every month he'd sent half his wages—more if he could afford it.

And every month he'd got a brief note thanking him for the payment.

Until the final one.

Well done, lad.

We're all square now and I wish you nothing but the best.

Dave

The note had meant a lot and he'd kept it.

'What's she like?' he asked now.

'Talkative,' Rachel said.

'Really?'

'Opinionated,' she elaborated. 'She's taking Dad shopping next week. Says she's sick of his old jumpers.'

'And he's agreed to go?'

'He's smitten.' Rachel rolled her eyes heavenwards. 'Smitten! I caught them kissing in the kitchen.'

Now, *that* he couldn't imagine, and Dominic felt his mouth gaped for a moment. 'And how do *you* feel about it?'

Rachel tightened her hand on her glass. Dominic had always made her examine things. He'd always asked how she felt. And now, just like thirteen years ago, she didn't know how to share how she felt, so she settled for the classic response.

'Fine.' Rachel shrugged. 'As long as he's happy.'

Only that wasn't quite true, and she could not entirely escape Dominic's piercing eyes. She could almost feel her superpower fading against the scrutiny of his gaze. It dawned on her that apart from her brothers, who didn't discuss such things, Dominic was the only person she knew who might understand the magnitude of her dad dating again.

'It's going to take a bit of getting used to,' she admitted.

'Has there been anyone else since your mum?'

Rachel found she was holding her breath, because in the past he had always been trying to get her to open up about her mum. He'd always slip her into conversation, when in the Walker household the subject of her mum had been strictly forbidden.

'No.' She gave a small shake of her head.

'So she's the first woman he's dated in twenty-six years?' Dominic said. 'Wow.'

Yes, wow, indeed…

It touched her that without asking he could

do the maths, that he still knew the dates and anniversaries that mattered so much to her.

'I think it's been going on for a while,' Rachel admitted.

'What makes you think that?'

'Just a couple of things that were said. I actually think she's angling to move in.'

'Good luck to her, then. I remember trying to stack that dishwasher…'

'Oh, it wasn't just you he had a go at about it,' Rachel assured him. 'I don't go near it. He's so set in his ways I just can't believe he's started dating.'

'She must be pretty special,' Dominic commented, 'to have got under that rhino hide of his.'

'Maybe…' she conceded.

He was making her laugh.

He was making her think.

But then, Dominic had always done that to her.

'Give her a chance, Rachel.'

'I am—but what if she does move in?' Rachel sighed. 'And what happens if…?' She stopped then, and blinked, because she hadn't aired her thoughts about this to anyone before. Even when they'd been together she'd kept most of her thoughts to herself.

'If they break up?'

'Yes.'

'You can't stop your dad getting hurt.'

'I know that.'

'At least she won't have to look far for a removal company.' Dominic laughed. 'God, remember when he moved us into the flat?'

Rachel wished he wouldn't reminisce, but she gave a little laugh to disguise her confusion at her fondness for the memories he evoked. 'I do.'

They'd actually had so little to move that it could have been done in a couple of car trips, but her dad had insisted on a lorry.

'That flat's actually up for sale.'

She'd passed the sign when she'd been at home, visiting her dad, but she didn't dare tell Dominic that she'd been tempted to go in and take a look, for old times' sake…

Rachel hadn't known it back then, of course, but both the best and worst times of her life had taken place in that flat.

* * *

Dominic bought them both another drink, and they reminisced for a dangerously long while.

About the flat.

About the café across the road.

About the best of times.

But not about the parts that hurt the most—and Dominic knew it was time to get to that.

'Do you want another drink,' he offered, 'or the menu?'

'No, no… I really ought to head off.' She drained the last of her juice. 'What is it that you want to ask me?'

'It's a bit sensitive.'

'It's fine,' she invited. 'Just ask.'

In another version of themselves, Dominic thought, he would take her hand. That was how things had worked for them. Except that wasn't appropriate now, so instead of holding her hand, he steepled his fingers and pushed himself to speak.

'The photos of Christopher that were taken at the hospital… I don't have any.'

'I'll get you some,' Rachel said hurriedly, wishing she had a sip of juice left, because her mouth was suddenly dry and she could hear the roar of her pulse in her ears as Dominic spoke on.

'I did attempt to get some from the hospital, but it's closed down and I hit a wall trying.'

She nodded. 'I'll have some copies made.'

'I don't want to upset you…' He tried to gauge her expression, but it was completely closed off. 'But I'd really appreciate it.'

'If you can give me a few days…?'

'Whenever you have time.'

She nodded again.

'Rachel…'

He knew, despite appearances, that she was hurting. He couldn't *not* take her hand—except she pulled her hand back and took herself completely out of bounds.

'I said I'd get them for you.'

Rachel knew she'd snapped, that she'd overreacted to his touch, but it was either that or break down.

Right now she was mourning not just the loss of her baby, but also all the moments they'd never shared—as a family, as a couple. So badly did she want to take Dominic's hand, take him back to her empty flat and go through those photos together. But they hadn't been able to accomplish that when they were married, so there was no chance now they were not.

She moved to stand. 'I really ought to go.'

'You're sure?' Dominic checked, and she nodded.

But of course it wasn't as simple as just getting up and walking out.

As if she were dressing for a North Pole expedition, on went her coat, the scarf and the hat. But, feeling his impatience, she omitted the gloves and stuffed them into her pocket instead.

'Don't you have a coat?' she asked as they headed out.

'No need. I'm driving,' Dominic said, though she noticed he had not offered her a lift home.

They walked out of the pub together and into the dark car park, both wondering how to end this rather awkward meeting.

Rachel did not recognise his mood. He stood taller than usual, if that was possible, and his expression was serious. Her own feelings were jumbled up after being asked to give him copies of the photos, and it was awkward to know how to say goodbye.

Though it should not be awkward because there was nothing to say—or rather, because there was so much to say that they did not know how to discuss. Their failed marriage and the baby they'd lost, the photos he didn't have and their working together, the attraction that still existed between them.

That persisted.

For, despite all the changes over the years, there *were* parts of Dominic she recognised.

Like the slight glaze that came to his eyes when he wanted her.

The way he stood just a smidge too close and dominated her space.

Or was it that she'd stepped a little closer into his?

And when he looked down at her, and she looked up at him, they both recognised the want in the other person's eyes.

It wasn't fair, Rachel thought. All desire for each other should have been returned with the divorce papers. Every shred of want should have been annulled.

Except it hadn't been.

He was smartly dressed, but end-of-day dishevelled, and he was hungry—she knew it as well as if he had told her himself. She simply knew. And, though he stood still, she also knew he was restless.

In another time they'd be kissing now.

In an older version of themselves they would not have been able to wait for each other's mouths until they were home…

'Are you getting the Tube?' Dominic asked gruffly, and she nodded. 'Then I'll say good-night here.'

'Sure.'

How to leave him, though?

A little wave? Rachel thought, but that seemed stupid.

A handshake, then? Even worse.

And, anyway, evidently they did not know how to *do* a handshake—because as his fingers met hers she looked down at their hands and saw they were entwined once again, and she could not bring herself to pull her hand away.

A small kiss, perhaps?

Before she knew what was happening, their touching hands led to moving in for a small kiss…

Except it was rather like testing the Christmas tree lights, not really expecting them to be working, but then being stunned by the blazing, breathtaking effect when they suddenly sparked into life.

The instant their lips met they were hurtled back to a time when touch had not been out of bounds. To a time when they had relished each other completely.

Her body lit like a flare, her senses jamming at the return to this bliss.

There was nothing tentative about this kiss.

It was harsh, and thorough, and when gravity wasn't enough to keep her standing, instead of holding her up he kissed her against the cold brick wall of the car park.

He pulled off her hat and it fell silently to the wet ground. He made her want sex in dark places as he filled her senses with his touch, his taste, his smell. His ragged breathing told her that he wanted the same. The frantic tangle of their tongues left them both suddenly desperate.

He went for her belt and parted the fabric of her coat, building to a kiss that was too much for a drink after work on a Monday.

It was a kiss that warned them they could never be just friends.

And then Dominic felt an unwelcome tap on his shoulder. Only it wasn't a person—it wasn't even his conscience. It was the unwelcome thought that they were hurtling towards an affair.

And Dominic, thanks to the less-than-gorgeous lessons of his parents' marriage, would never go there.

'For God's sake, Rachel!' he accused as he pulled back. 'What the hell are you doing?'

'Me?' she shot back, because he knew he hadn't exactly been unwilling. 'It takes two!'

'Yes, but I'm not the one who's engaged.'

Dominic was furious with himself.

While a torrid affair was way down on his list of wants, messing up her life again was way more abhorrent.

'Go home,' he told her.

He looked down at her coat that he had parted, at her tousled hair and freshly kissed mouth. He wished for an eraser that might somehow unsex her—if there were such a thing. For if Rachel had ever come home to *him* looking like that, he'd have known in an instant.

He reached for her belt and started to tie it. 'This never happened,' he said. 'This is never going to happen ag—'

'Gordon and I broke up,' Rachel cut in, and felt his hands still. 'I ended it last week.'

He looked at her then—right at her. And she rather hoped they could get back to kissing...get back to a moment ago, when she had been swept away by the power of their connection.

But now she had cleared the air and finally told him.

Except the bark of his response to the news startled her.

'Why would you go and do that?'

Rachel didn't know what to say.

But that didn't matter because Dominic had plenty to say!

'Don't do this, Rachel.'

'Do what?'

'Don't throw away a relationship over me…'

'I didn't.'

'I mean it, Rachel. We will not be getting back together. I have *nothing* to offer you, as far as the future's concerned.'

His words were so blunt, his statement so absolute, that something inside her shrivelled. And as she stood there being told—yes, *told*—that there was absolutely no chance for them, that marriage and babies were the very last thing he wanted, she knew that hope had just died. The little flicker of hope she hadn't even known existed had just been doused.

Embarrassment and anger kicked her into damage control mode and she gave a mocking laugh. '*You?* You really think I threw away a three-year relationship over you? What happened to you, Dominic? When did you get so arrogant?'

He let go of her completely then, and there was only one word going through Rachel's head: *deny, deny, deny.*

'Did it not enter your head that I could end

a relationship without factoring *you* in?' She breathed in hard and found some strength. 'Gordon and I had only just moved in together, and I realised almost straight away that we'd made a mistake.'

That, at least, was the truth.

'Fair enough,' Dominic said. 'But, Rachel, I have to be sure. Because you and I…' He looked down at her and she recalled the pain and the hell of the end of their marriage. 'We didn't work.'

'Obviously.'

'And, despite what I might have said before, I do want you to be happy. It just won't be with me. And so if my presence *did* have any impact on your decision, I suggest you go back to your fiancé and patch things up…'

'I would never use him like that, Dominic.' She blinked as she tried to fathom him. 'You seem to prefer that I be engaged.'

'I'd *prefer*,' Dominic clipped, 'that you'd never come back into my life.'

It was a horrible thing to say.

And as she turned and walked off Dominic knew he didn't really mean it.

After all, he'd tried to get in touch—not once, but twice over the years.

And now Rachel Walker had arrived back in his life with a pile of excess baggage—an awful lot of which belonged to him.

And it hurt to examine it.

CHAPTER SIX

THAT KISS SHOULD never have happened, Rachel knew. On so many levels, it should never have taken place.

For it had awoken her to him all over again.

The constant smouldering burn that had never quite died out had been reignited.

She didn't like him now, though, Rachel insisted to herself. This new, arrogant Dominic did not appeal.

And it was starting to show.

'Is your ex the redhead down in Emergency?' Richard asked Dominic after a particularly tense afternoon in Resus. 'Rachel?'

'How did you know it was her?' he asked.

'Because the two of you barely speak.'

'I told you,' Dominic said. 'We've agreed to be professional and polite.'

'With extra ice added?'

'Well, how are we supposed to be?' Dominic snapped. He was doing rather a lot of that of late. 'We're hardly going to be friends.'

But he knew it couldn't go on like this.

He sighed and headed back to the department, for he had to sort things out.

Dominic did *not* want to be in lust with his ex-wife. And certainly he did not want a relationship with her. He was well aware of how badly it had worked out the first time.

Despite Rachel's protests to the contrary, he was still silently panicked that she'd broken off her engagement because of him.

And there she was, with a long-sleeved top on under her scrubs. Because Rachel was *always* cold.

'We need to speak,' Dominic said. 'Alone.'

'This is becoming a habit, Dominic. Won't it look odd?' Rachel said. 'Us hiding in the drug room or the linen cupboard?'

'Can't you go for a break?'

'I'm not due for one. Just say what you have to here,' Rachel insisted.

But when he stood there silently, refusing to back down, with a sigh she led them to an empty cubicle, where she pulled the curtain to give them some privacy.

'I'm sorry about what I said the other night,' he started. 'I was shocked that you and Gordon had broken up and concerned—'

'I don't need your concern.'

'Let me finish,' Dominic said. 'I was concerned that my being here might have factored into your decision to end things with him.'

'Well, it didn't.'

'Good—because it's very clear that we want different things. I like the single life. The only thing I want to be married to is my career, and the last thing I want is a family. In fact…' He took a deep breath and knew the time had come to tell her what he had done. 'I've made sure it can never happen. I had a vasectomy some years ago.'

'Dominic,' Rachel said coolly. 'We were divorced thirteen years ago. You don't have to run your contraceptive methods by me.'

Ha! she thought, laughing in her head at her cool response. *Beat that.*

He did.

'I might have had to the other night,' Dominic said, his eyes never leaving her face as he moved one dangerous step closer, nudging into her personal space.

He took her hand and for a moment she honestly thought he was going to place it on his crotch.

'Because if I hadn't stopped things when I did we might have ended up doing it against the wall.'

'You really think so?'

'I *know* so.'

Rachel thought she deserved a cape, tiara and a wand—because she didn't even blush, despite picturing him doing just that.

The scent of their arousal was in the air she breathed, and his mouth—*that* mouth—was a mere arch of her neck away. But she didn't step back, determined to hold both her position and his eyes.

'Dominic, it was a kiss for old times' sake. Please don't go reading more into it than that.'

The audacity of him!

She shook his hand off hers. 'I'm certainly

not rushing around looking for a replacement fiancé.'

'Good.'

'And while we're *sharing*,' Rachel said, 'the reason Gordon and I broke up is because I didn't want what happened to me to happen to him. He's a good person.'

She watched Dominic's eyebrows draw together in confusion at that.

'And I know, better than most, how it feels to be married to someone who doesn't really want to be married to you.'

'What are you talking about?' His eyes widened incredulously at her words. 'I went and told your dad the day I found out about the baby. I asked him for his permission to marry you the same night. I deferred university. I worked two jobs. I even offered to move in with your dad…'

He shook his head, clearly furious at her take on their marriage.

'You didn't love me, Dominic.'

'No.'

He seemed hurt, angry, but the one thing she knew was that they could not go back down the path of *them* again.

'And do you know why?' he asked.

She rather felt that she didn't want to know, but he let her have it.

'Because apart from in bed, Rachel, I found you to be cold.'

Dominic knew that was below the belt. But this woman brought out the worst in him, as well as the best in him, and her return had made him relive every last hurt again.

Trying to reach out to someone who constantly pushed you away. Crying alone in the shower for your baby, then walking into a bedroom where your wife had already turned to face the wall. Knowing the pain you had caused her…knowing what you had both lost.

And even now, when he'd hurt her again, she barely blinked.

'It must be catching, then,' Rachel said, and walked off.

Rachel knew it now for a fact. Dominic Hadley had never loved her—which meant she had been right to guard her heart.

Luckily there were only ten minutes or so left of her shift, and within the hour she had let herself into her flat. Without even taking off her coat, she went into the bedroom, opened up a drawer and took out a faded cream folder.

The first thing to fall out was her wedding ring, which she'd once so proudly worn. And then she took out an exercise book she'd kept from school—one that Dominic had written his phone number on. There were lots of little messages he'd written to her in class too, but she could read the true intent behind them now.

What time will your dad be back?

So they could have sex.

I got them!

Condoms—so they could have sex.

Has it finished yet?

Her period—so they could have sex.

Teenaged Dominic Hadley really had had sex on his mind—and fool that she was, she'd confused it with love.

Well, no more.

She fed the exercise book into the shredder, page after page, and cried bitter tears as she did it. Then she took out their wedding photo, but could not bring herself to shred that.

There were also certificates—marriage, birth, death and divorce—and those papers were such a neat summing up of their relationship that she could not bear to look at them properly.

And then she got to the photos Dominic wanted. It twisted like a knife in her gut to look at them, but they also made her smile.

There was one photo of the three of them, sitting on the bed, with Rachel holding Christopher and Dominic's arm around her.

And there were several of just Christopher. She touched his pinched little face and open mouth, his long slender fingers, the fine fuzz of hair on his head.

She would get these reprinted and give them to Dominic, and then all would finally be said and done between them.

No, there had been no need to take off her coat, because in minutes she was out of the door again.

Always be kind.

It was a saying often bandied about, but that evening, when someone tutted as she knocked into them while lining up to print off the photos for Dominic, the snap of a stranger's temper nearly had Rachel giving in and turning to run for home. That single terse 'tut' just about had her heading for King's Cross Station and the first train back to Sheffield, but instead she got the photos copied and was soon back at her flat.

Job done.

When she'd given them to Dominic there would be nothing more to discuss, no more conversations to be had, and the subject of their past would be entirely closed.

Rachel sealed the envelope and labelled it *Photos*, and then put it in her bag. Now she just had to give them to him when the chance arose.

Except it never arose.

For the first time in her career, Rachel started to put her hand up to work in Minor Injuries rather than the main section of Emergency or Resus.

There was less chance of seeing Dominic there.

'How did you do this?' Rachel asked as she pulled on gloves and peeled back the tea towel wrapped around the hand of a delightful elderly woman who had brought herself to The Primary on a bus.

'Peeling and cutting up pumpkins,' said Miss Tate. 'I make soup for the homeless, and pumpkin soup is supposed to be easy. But, Nurse, they're really hard to cut.'

'I bet they are.'

'But it's a flexible soup.'

'Flexible?' Rachel checked as she examined the deep cut and saw the exposed tendons.

'Vegan, gluten-free, nut-free…' Miss Tate reeled them all off. 'And don't get me started on the health and safety regulations. It's wearing gloves that caused this to happen—I couldn't get a grip of the knife. In my day you just put a bone in a pot, but it's a complicated affair now, making soup.'

As well as hazardous, Rachel thought, picturing these shaky arthritic hands wrestling with a large knife and a pumpkin.

She looked at her patient, and saw that Miss Tate was a little bit grey and was sweating. 'It's rather a long wait,' Rachel said, 'but I can get you on a gurney and lying down…'

'I don't mind waiting.'

'Well, let's make you as comfortable as we can. Is there anyone I can call?'

'No need to trouble anyone.'

Rachel looked up as the curtain swished open and saw May.

'I just need a word, Rachel,' she said.

She paused when she saw what Rachel was dealing with and, instead of insisting on having a conversation, gave Rachel a hand with Miss Tate, chatting away about the pumpkin disaster as they got her up onto a trolley and into a gown.

'Chilli flakes are the secret ingredient to a good soup,' Miss Tate said.

'Ah, but I don't like it too spicy.' May shook her head.

'No, just a little pinch—it brings out all the flavours.'

'Could you not roast the pumpkin first and *then* cut it up?' May suggested.

'Oh!' Miss Tate dwelled on that suggestion for a moment. 'I think that might work. *Roast* pumpkin soup…that sounds very nice.'

With the soup and the patient sorted for now, May pulled Rachel aside. 'We'll miss you tomorrow night,' she said.

Rachel had taken her name off the list for the ED night out. She had come up with loads of excuses to justify it, but mainly it was because she did not want to see Dominic socially.

'I've got your deposit for you,' May said, handing her an envelope.

'I thought it was non-refundable.'

'I always say that,' May admitted, 'but we've got plenty going, so the numbers are fine. It's a shame, though. I was looking forward to meeting your man… What's his name?'

'Gordon.' Rachel smiled, because if she'd told May once, then she'd told her fifty times. Still, there was something she *hadn't* yet told her and there was no time like the present. 'May, Gordon and I have broken up.'

'Oh, my dear! When did that happen?'

'A little while ago. I didn't say anything at the time, because, well…'

'Of course not. You needed time to process it.' May was serious now. 'Does it change anything? I mean, I know you moved to London because of his job. Are we going to lose you, Rachel?'

'I don't honestly know, May.' Rachel told her the truth she was coming to know. 'The flat's too expensive for only me. If I stay then I'm going to have to find somewhere else.'

And, while she liked London, with Dominic so near it was hell. If she was going to have to find somewhere else to live, why not in Sheffield, where her family and friends were?

Well away from Dominic.

She couldn't hide in Minor Injuries for ever. And Rachel knew she *was* hiding.

'You're still on a trial, Rachel, so you only have to give a week's notice, but for what it's worth, I'd be very sorry to lose you.'

'Thank you.'

'Listen,' May said. 'Do you want a shift tomorrow night? I'm having trouble covering the department, what with everyone coming for this night out, and I've had someone ring in sick.'

'I'd love to,' Rachel said. She'd been about to ask May if there were any extra shifts, but the overtime for a Saturday night would certainly help.

For now.

Rachel knew she would have to make a decision soon about staying.

And, despite May's kind words, it was starting to look very unlikely.

CHAPTER SEVEN

DOMINIC KNEW HE had to get Rachel out of his head. And he decided it would be best to do it in a way he knew only too well. He would lose himself in a woman's body.

Since Rachel had been back on the scene there had been none of that.

None.

He knew Rachel had put her name down to be at this social event tonight, but he had decided it was time to set new ground rules. Tonight, he fully intended to rediscover the joys of being single and commitment-free and to indulge in some completely meaningless sex.

Dominic was usually very good at that.

'Dominic! Over here!'

His name was being called from a couple of directions, but Tara waved for him to take the empty seat she had kept for him. They weren't an item, although they'd got it on at times, but instead of joining her, he gave a vague nod as his eyes scanned the room.

Rachel wasn't here, he realised.

He ignored the gritting of his jaw when the flash of red hair, which his eyes reluctantly sought, didn't appear.

Good! he told himself, refusing to acknowledge that the thud in his chest might be born of disappointment rather than relief.

Good, he said again, to himself. It was excellent that his ex-wife wasn't here, policing his moves.

Except instead of heading over to sit beside Tara, he moved towards the empty seat next to Jordan. They went way back, and had been through medical school together. Dominic had even been best man at his wedding.

'No Heather?'

'Nope.'

'Mind if I join you, then?'

'Of course. The babysitter cancelled,' Jordan explained as Dominic took a seat, 'and frankly I don't blame her.'

'Are the twins still wild, then?'

'Completely.' Jordan nodded. 'And Nicholas is following their lead.'

'Sounds like you need a night off,' Dominic said.

He knew very well that Jordan was stressed about some upcoming changes to the paediatric unit, as well as bogged down with work, so adding a young family to that mix must only increase the burden.

'I don't know how you do it all.'

'Oh, I wouldn't have it any other way,' Jordan said as the starter was served.

The *saganaki* was the best Dominic had tasted, yet he pushed it around his plate, for once not particularly hungry.

The whole meal was delectable, but Dominic didn't clear his plate. He wasn't alone—surprisingly Jordan, who loved his food too, didn't finish, but unlike Dominic, he could explain why.

'I promised Heather I'd bring home a curry.'

And just when Dominic was starting to question what on earth he was doing, talking toddlers and happy marriages with Jordan when there was Tara pouting petulantly and no doubt waiting for him to take her home, a memory pierced his mind… Ending his shift at the bar and grabbing a curry—because of course he was starving, but also a very pregnant Rachel had had a bit of a craving for it.

As well as a craving for him.

The memory was so vivid, so real, he could almost *feel* the happiness that had existed between them as he'd walked into their freezing flat. He'd grabbed some plates from the kitchenette, walked into their ice box of a bedroom, holding up the bag of food like a trophy, then stripped off and climbed into their warm bed.

They'd eaten as if they'd been starved for a week, tearing at the naan bread, scooping up the curry and devouring it. And then had come the best bit. Rachel loved *gulab jamun*—sweet syrupy balls that they generally didn't order—but that night he'd surprised her.

They'd already been turned on, but her groan as she'd eaten one had driven him wild, and a gorgeous wrestle had ensued.

Rachel, eight months pregnant and on top of him, sweet, sticky sex, with syrup everywhere, and an orgasm that had had him seeing stars...

It had been followed by a kind of clarity and peace he'd not known since, with his difficult, fickle woman, who revealed so little and only very occasionally blossomed and opened up—but only to him.

And later, with both of Rachel's cravings satisfied, they'd lain there, feeling the kicks of their baby and trying to decide on a name.

It had perhaps been the most pure and simple happiness he had ever known.

'Okay,' Jordan said suddenly, breaking into his thoughts. 'I can't not tell you.'

Dominic turned. 'Tell me what?'

'Heather's expecting.' Jordan beamed. 'We're beside ourselves because we're so pleased.'

Dominic looked at his friend, who was smiling delightedly at news that would have had Dominic running for the hills. *Four!* Four children, by his rapid calculation all under four, including the terrible twins! Yet Jordan had always said he wanted a big family, and he and Heather were, from all Dominic could tell, as in love now as they had been on their wedding day.

More so, even.

'Congratulations,' Dominic said. 'You're a lucky bastard.'

'Oh, I know I am,' Jordan said.

Suddenly Dominic wanted what he himself had once known. He wanted that pure and simple happiness again.

The meal ended and it was then that the party kicked off. This would usually have been the time when Dominic would have really started to enjoy himself. But this evening he just could not get into the swing of it—and it had nothing to do with the sparkling water he was drinking.

'Hey, Dominic!'

Tara was waving him over to the dance floor, but he had absolutely no desire to go over and join her. No desire in that direction at all.

'You're quiet, Dominic,' Jordan commented. 'Do you want a drink?'

'I'll just stick to water, thanks,' Dominic said.

'Is everything okay?'

Dominic glanced up and frowned at Jordan's enquiry. 'Of course.'

'Only with Rachel working in Emergency…'

'What?' Dominic was furious. 'Did Richard tell you?'

'No,' Jordan said. '*You* did—a couple of years ago.'

Dominic closed his eyes and drummed his fingers on the table. The less said about that night the better.

'You had Heather looking her up on social media, remember—?'

'Don't let on that you know,' Dominic cut in. 'She's adamant that she doesn't want it to get out.' Christ, it was like trying to keep the lid on Pandora's Box. 'I mean it, Jordan.'

'I won't say anything,' Jordan said, 'but I'm here if you want to talk.'

Jordan left it there, and said he was getting up for one quick dance before heading home.

The Emergency Department certainly knew how to party. People were actually dancing on the tables now, and Dominic was being urged to join in.

Only Tara's laugh suddenly grated on him, and he didn't like the possessive way she'd placed a hand on his arm, as if it were up to her to collect him for dancing, so he brushed it off and politely declined.

Tara's nostrils did that pinched thing—not that Dominic noticed as he headed for the bar and ordered another sparkling water, wondering what the hell was wrong with him.

Since Rachel's return to his life all other women seemed to have lost their appeal.

Although sex had never been as good as it had been between him and Rachel.

She had loved it.

He had loved it.

They had loved it.

Except for that awful first time.

He was laughing quietly to himself about that when he heard a crash and, turning around, saw that a table had collapsed—thanks to the weight of the people doing an impromptu Greek dance on top of it.

There should be no better place to be injured than at an Emergency Department party, but it meant an awful lot of people jostling to be in charge.

'I'm the only one sober,' Dominic pointed out as he took over. But one look at Jordan's shoulder told him this would require more than a simple sling. In fact, it was a nasty injury.

'We'd better head back to The Primary,' Dominic said, as he fashioned a sling with his tie and put Jordan's jacket on him back to front, buttoning it up to hold his arm securely in place.

'I'll come with you,' Tara offered.

'No need,' Dominic said, because she was seriously starting to annoy him.

There was no need. He escorted Jordan out to his car and drove him to The Primary.

It was pouring with rain, and so, rather than using his priority parking spot, he pulled into the forecourt. 'Wait there,' he told Jordan, rather needlessly. 'I'll go and find a wheelchair.'

The place was in its usual state of Saturday night chaos, so he knew there was little chance of finding a wheelchair, a gurney or anything useful.

Though there *was* Rachel.

She had on that long-sleeved top under her scrubs, and her gorgeous hair was in a high ponytail. She was the best thing to have happened to him this Saturday night.

But he could never accuse Rachel of being needy, because far from waving and smiling when she saw him, she gave a slight eye-roll as she came over.

'What happened?'

'I couldn't stay away from the place,' Dominic quipped. But she didn't even reward his pale joke with a smile. 'Jordan fell—he's fractured his right clavicle. I need a wheelchair but I can't find one.'

She left him standing as she went and got one.

'Thanks,' he said when she returned, and went to take it.

But Rachel didn't let the handles go. 'I'll come with you.'

'I can manage. I got him into the car.'

'And how many fractured clavicles have you got *out* of a car?'

None.

'I thought you were going to the do tonight?' Dominic commented as they walked out of the department.

'I didn't know I had to run my social calendar by you.'

'Fair enough,' Dominic conceded, and then admitted to himself that he'd missed her being there tonight. That despite all his earlier chat, Rachel was the only woman he'd wanted to see.

Dominic drove a low-slung sports car, but it clearly did nothing to impress her.

'Even I'd have trouble getting out of that,' Rachel muttered as they approached, but she dropped the attitude as soon as the car door opened.

'Hey,' she said, and smiled to Jordan even as she tried to map out his exit. 'What happened?'

'The Zorba dancing,' Jordan said through gritted teeth as his phone bleeped. 'Heather's been calling but I can't get to my phone. My wife,' he added, for Rachel's benefit.

'Why don't you speak to her when you're a bit more comfortable?' Rachel suggested. 'For now, let's focus on getting you out of the car.'

'I'm sorry about all this,' Jordan said. 'I've had a bit too much to drink…'

'It's fine.'

'Heather's going to freak.'

'Hey,' Rachel said, 'she's only going to freak because she'll be worried about you. Let's get you into the department.' She looked over to Dominic. 'Go into the driver's seat—you can support him from there when he turns.'

Zaima, the night sister on duty, joined them with a porter, and then Ross, the ED registrar on for the night shift, came out armed with a green whistle, which Jordan sucked on as they attempted extraction.

But every move proved agonising for him.

'Why didn't you call an ambulance?' Zaima said to Dominic when they failed the second time they'd tried.

'Because we'd still be waiting for it to arrive!' Dominic replied tartly, though he was beginning to wish he had. 'I'm sure the paramedics have got plenty to do on a Saturday night.'

'So have I!' Zaima retorted, in an equally tart tone.

Then Rachel asked Jordan to lean forward, and with Dominic assisting from the rear, she and Zaima lifted his feet. Soon they had him turned, and his feet on the ground, and then he was in the wheelchair and finally inside the ED.

Dominic went and moved his car.

* * *

'I'll get the receptionist to come and take your details,' Rachel said as she wheeled Jordan into a cubicle. 'Let's get you into a gown.'

It was indeed a nasty fracture, and he was given an IV and analgesics before they even tried to get him up onto a trolley.

When Jordan was finally comfortable Ross came in and examined him. 'How soon can we get him up for an X-ray?' he asked.

'We've got two portable chests waiting, and an urgent C-spine,' Zaima responded.

And whatever else had come in in the meantime.

'I can take him,' Dominic offered, as he came in and took a seat on a stool at the nurses' station.

Rachel shook her head. 'He needs a nurse with him, given he's had analgesics.'

'I'm sure I can manage—and, no, before you ask, I haven't been drinking.'

'It's policy,' Zaima said.

And policy would be adhered to—even if sitting on the hard chairs outside X-Ray an hour later with Dominic was the last place she wanted to be.

'How long will we be here?' Dominic asked.

'As long as it takes,' Rachel said.

He looked over to Jordan, who, thanks to the analgesics, was comfortable and fast asleep. She went over and checked the pulse in the arm affected by the fracture.

Jordan stirred and opened his eyes. 'I'm really sorry.'

'Jordan, it's fine,' Rachel said, and gave him the latest update. 'Heather's sorting out a babysitter and is on her way.'

But that only served to distress him.

'No, no…' Jordan said.

'They couldn't get a babysitter for tonight.' Dominic didn't exactly whisper, but he said it in low tones for Rachel's ears and then addressed Jordan. 'I'll call Heather now and tell her that I'll stay with you.'

'Will you tell her that you'll drive me home?'

'Let's see what the X-rays show,' Dominic answered carefully, because he was already certain that Jordan was going to be headed for Theatre, rather than home. 'I'll call her now.'

'Thanks,' Jordan said. 'He's a good friend,' he told Rachel, and then tried to focus on her. His eyes, thanks to all the morphine, were little pinpoints. 'He made a terrible husband, I'll bet, but he's a good friend.'

'Try and get some sleep,' Rachel said gently, impressing herself with how calm and gentle she kept her voice.

She gave him a nice smile as he closed his eyes and fell asleep.

'Good God!' she said to Dominic as he returned from calling Heather. 'Did you go into the doctors' mess with a megaphone and tell them all your ex-wife was working in the Emergency Department?'

Dominic had the audacity to laugh. 'People talk, Rachel.'

'Well, *I* don't.'

'Normal people, then. Look, Jordan's the most discreet person—honestly, Rachel. He knows me from way back. We went to med school together.'

'Well, when he's sobered up, would you

please remind your friend that I don't want this getting out?'

She was cross, but Dominic's laughter was infectious, and she found that she was smiling and feeling just a little bit warm on the inside. Their marriage had mattered enough to Dominic that he'd had to share it with his friend.

'I'll remind him,' Dominic said as the radiographer came out.

Jordan was wheeled in and Rachel went with him.

'Busy?' the radiographer asked her in a dry tone.

'Just a bit.'

Jordan was lovely and co-operative, and didn't need to be told to hold his breath when the chest films were taken, but he did whimper at some of the positions required for other images.

'Stay nice and still,' the radiographer said as she and Rachel stood behind the lead screen. 'As still as you can…'

Rachel frowned, because Jordan was suddenly restless and pulling the film from under his arm.

'Jordan?' Rachel came out from behind the screen. 'Jordan!'

He was struggling to breathe. She took his pulse and found it was irregular, and saw he was starting to turn blue. The radiographer hit the emergency button that would turn on a strobe light above the room and also in the ED, to indicate that urgent help was required.

'Get Dominic!' Rachel called to the radiographer as she laid Jordan flat.

Dominic glanced up and saw the flashing light. It must have been set off by accident, he told himself as he looked to its source.

Jordan had a fractured clavicle, for God's sake.

But years of experience had Dominic standing, ready to dash in.

He strode into X-Ray and was met with the precariousness of life.

Jordan was blue and Rachel was using an Ambu bag to attempt to breathe life into him. The radiographer was attaching the defibrillator and also an oxygen saturation probe to his finger.

'What happened?' Dominic asked as he took the stethoscope from Rachel's neck.

'He became agitated,' Rachel said. 'Sudden collapse. Should we get him round to Resus?'

Jordan's oxygen saturations were dire, and as Dominic listened to his breath sounds he figured out what had happened. 'Tension pneumothorax,' he said, taking a ten-mil syringe from the emergency trolley. 'I'm going to do a needle thoracostomy here.'

He really must have nerves of steel, he thought, because he shut out the fact that it was probably his closest friend he was stabbing with a syringe. But when there was a popping sound, and the hiss of trapped air being released, he let out a breath of relief of his own.

'What the hell—?' Zaima said as she ran in. 'Oh, Jordan…'

It was horrible—horrible for everyone. But soon they had him back in Resus, though he was flailing and conscious by the time they got there.

'Stay still, Jordan,' Dominic ordered, his eyes like a hawk's, taking it all in as he attempted to stay back and let the team work on his friend.

Soon they had him stabilised, and Dominic took on the less-than-pleasant task of calling Heather to update her.

Dominic didn't look forward to that call one bit.

But Jordan was a lot more comfortable now, with heavy-duty pain relief and a chest tube in, and he would be headed for Theatre as soon as a slot opened up—although they were seriously backed up.

'We might try and get him onto the ward,' Zaima had said. 'At least then he can wait in a comfortable bed.'

Rachel was checking Jordan's blood pressure when Dominic came back from calling Heather. Jordan's face was the colour of putty.

'How is she?' Jordan asked groggily.

'She's okay,' Dominic said. 'Her mother's on her way to look after the children, and then Heather will be here. I said I'd stay with you till she comes.'

'Is she very upset?'

'She's fine. Just annoyed that you didn't bring home her curry…'

He was trying to keep things light, but the truth was it had taken a lot to calm Heather down. He didn't want to stress out Jordan with all that.

The second he'd mentioned the curry, Dominic had glanced over at Rachel and caught her eyes. The porcelain skin that never flushed suddenly had, and Dominic knew that Rachel was remembering that long-ago night before it had all gone so wrong for them.

Of course, neither Jordan nor Zaima had the slightest clue of the history that danced between them…

As Dominic waited for Heather to arrive, he sat by Jordan and watched Rachel work.

Not in an obvious way—more he just sat by Jordan, who was dozing, and she appeared now and then to check his obs, or he caught sight of her wheeling a patient past. She looked ever more tired and pale as the night progressed, and the band holding her ponytail slipped lower.

He wondered why, with all the painted beauty available to him tonight, it was still her.

Had always been her, really.

There had never been another woman who absorbed him as much, and he pondered how her bland expression as she steered a huge singing drunk man in a wheelchair through the department could make him smile.

The queen of deadpan, he'd once called her.

She never fully revealed her thoughts and it had driven him crazy at times.

At other times, though, he had relished the game of guessing what was going on in her mind. The thrill of the chase and the flirtation had never been better with anyone else than it had been between them.

And now it had started again.

She stopped by the trolley where Jordan lay, still sleeping. 'He's first on the list for the morning,' she told Dominic. 'You might as well head home.'

'I said I'd stay till Heather gets here—though it won't be for a while, as her mother lives a good few hours away.'

‘Well, I’m going on my break,’ she told him. ‘Do you want to share my roll?’

‘I would love to share your roll, Rachel.’

It was just a cheese-and-salad roll, with a generous layer of Henderson’s Relish, and she sliced it into two in the unit’s kitchen.

They had shared many such rolls in the past.

On the day he had started at Rachel’s school, instead of heading to the dining room, he had sat with her under a vast oak and she had shared her homemade lunch with him.

Now she made two mugs of builder’s tea—dark and strong and exactly how he had come to like it. And as he watched her squeeze the teabags and flick them into the bin, he knew not a single person watching would even guess they were flirting. Even if cameras were trained on them and their moves were being analysed, no one would be able to tell.

But they were.

She carried the plates and he carried the mugs, and they went into the large, deserted staff room and sat down opposite each other.

'Still like the relish, I see,' he said in his fake northern accent, after he'd taken a bite and tasted the spicy fruity tang that was a staple in the Walker household—well, everywhere in Sheffield, really.

'Aye!' Rachel said.

'Reminds me of the lunch breaks I'd take when I worked with your dad.'

'I am sorry about that.'

'About what?'

'About my family. They gave you a hard time.'

'Not really,' he dismissed, but then he laughed mirthlessly, because the Walkers weren't exactly sensitive New Age guys and it had been one hell of a time when he'd worked with them. 'Yeah, it was pretty rough—but that said, they were just being protective. I did get you pregnant; they were never going to go easy on me.'

And this time he didn't shrug, but told her a truth instead.

'That year of working with them did me a lot of favours. For all his blundering ways, your dad's actually very good at small talk.' He gave a soft laugh of recall. 'He could chat to anyone,' Dominic said. 'I mean, moving house is one of the most stressful times of people's lives, yet your dad would nail it each and every time, and some of it rubbed off on me.'

'Really?'

Dominic nodded, then watched as she lay back in her seat and closed her eyes—not to sleep, but to sigh. 'What a night…'

'I know,' Dominic agreed.

In the scheme of things, a tension pneumothorax on a Saturday night was something they were well used to, but it felt very different when it was a colleague and friend.

'How was Heather?'

'Terrified,' Dominic admitted. 'I tried to play it down a bit, but she's a doctor herself. She knows it was touch and go for a moment.'

'Not with you there,' she said, opening her eyes and looking right at him. 'Your hand didn't even shake.'

'Well, I wouldn't be much good if it did. I just had to shut it all out and focus on the task, and then panic afterwards…' Then he admitted the truth. 'He'd just told me that Heather's pregnant again.'

'God!'

'I'd literally just told him what a lucky bastard he was...'

'Really?' Rachel said. 'And there I was thinking you'd be giving him the name of your vasectomy surgeon.'

It was a little dig, but it made both of them smile.

He'd never expected her to smile about it...

In fact, Rachel was surprised to discover that what she felt was the oddest sensation of sweet relief. Perhaps, she told herself, it was because it took any future for them—even if it was only in her imaginings—right off the table. Because more than anything Rachel wanted to be a mother some day.

Only that wasn't quite it.

She was looking right at him.

Still.

And the news that he'd had a vasectomy somehow made sex—well, just about sex.

It was actually quite liberating.

It all boiled down to desire.

And that desire was there.

Zaima came in then and broke the spell. She had come for a coffee, rather than her meal break, she said, though Rachel was sure it was actually to find out all the gossip from the Emergency team's night out.

'Who else was up on the tables?' she asked Dominic. 'Was May?'

'No!' Dominic grinned.

'What about Louise from Maternity?'

'I don't think so,' Dominic said.

Usually that would have been something he'd notice, thought Rachel—because Louise, a midwife on Maternity, was stunning.

Zaima pushed for more gossip by bribing him with salt-and-vinegar crisps. 'What about Tara?'

'She was there.' He nodded.

And Rachel was horrified to feel a slight twitch of her nose. Her superpower was fading… But then, it had never been put to the test against the thought of Dominic dancing with another woman before.

Zaima didn't pick up on the tension between Rachel and Dominic because there was nothing to see.

The chemistry belonged entirely to them.

Rachel's internal radar was tuned with precision to him, and she knew, even though he chatted and ate crisps, that his little pauses before answering Zaima's questions were down to her presence.

Indeed, Dominic *was* having trouble focusing on the conversation—because it was killing him not to have Rachel again. And it was killing him to work alongside her.

No, things could not continue as they were. The fault line was shifting. But he was more than happy to suffer any collision that might be ahead if it meant he got to be with Rachel again.

He glanced over to where she sat, watching the television and sipping her tea, as if butter wouldn't melt in her mouth, but he was certain of the fire that was growing between them.

'I'd better get back,' Zaima said.

Rachel glanced up at the clock to see how much of her meal break she had left. 'I'll be back in ten.'

She turned back to the television, but the image on it seemed blurry and she had no idea what else was being said, such was her awareness of Dominic in the room.

'Do you ever think of us?' Dominic asked suddenly.

Rachel swallowed. She wanted to give a dismissive laugh, as if that might shut him down, except it would be a blatant lie. 'Sometimes.'

'Because I've been thinking about us a lot of late,' Dominic pushed, 'and I think you've been thinking about us too.'

'What part of us?' Rachel asked dryly, and continued staring ahead. 'The arguments, the bills, the—?'

'Not those parts.'

She swallowed again. She was tempted to pick up her mug and walk out, but then she turned and looked at Dominic, thirteen years older and somehow all the sexier for it. Which was incredible, because there had not been a single thing she would have changed about him back then. Yet here he was, pale from lack of sleep, with dark shadows under his eyes and unshaven, and he still made her weak with wanting.

'It would be a mistake,' Rachel said, talking about the sex that now seemed inevitable.

'Perhaps,' Dominic conceded. 'However, of all my regrets—and with you there are many—one of the biggest is that I can't remember the last time we did it.'

She was startled.

For once she was actually startled—and not because of what he'd said, more because she had been thinking the same thing.

'Neither can I,' she admitted.

Their sex life had died with their baby. It hadn't felt right to reach out for comfort. For solace. For the moment of peace their love-making gave. She hadn't known how. And on top of all that for Rachel there had been a sense of impending doom that their marriage was about to end.

But she also hated it that she couldn't remember their last time.

She'd tried to think back, but they'd been at it all the time. If she'd known that it was the last time she'd have treated the moment, the memory, with infinite care.

'It might complicate things,' she said now.

'Or it might clear the air,' Dominic said. 'I want to remember our last time.'

There was a warning there—that it would be a one-off—even as he invited her to play this dangerous game.

She could have chosen to take offence, but she didn't, for if she decided to give in to her perpetual desire for him, then it most certainly would be for the last time.

She gave him a smile, but no answer, collecting her mug and returning to work.

Rachel had made her decision.

Richard knew about them, his wife probably knew, and Jordan knew. Very soon everyone would know…

She simply could not work in a goldfish bowl where their failed marriage was gossiped about.

And she could not move on with her life alongside him.

She was leaving The Primary.

Heather arrived at just after seven in the morning, and Rachel walked her up to the ward to which Jordan had been transferred.

'Of all the irresponsible things to do!' Heather said as they took the lift. 'What on earth was he doing, dancing on a table?'

'Letting off steam?' Rachel ventured.

'Killing himself, more like,' Heather said, letting off a little steam of her own.

She was clearly frantic and scared as the ward nurse pointed them in the direction of his bed, in a four-bed pod near the nurses' station.

Dominic was sitting in a chair beside him, but jumped up when he saw Heather and gave her a hug.

'He's going to be fine,' Dominic said.

And Heather stopped being cross as soon as she saw her husband, groggy from medication and with tubes and drips everywhere.

'Oh, Jordan,' she sobbed. '*Look* at you!'

'Heather...' Jordan said. 'I'm so sorry.'

'Stop that now,' Heather said as she hugged him. 'It's just rotten luck.'

It made Rachel feel teary, and she wasn't quite sure why. Their intimacy and obvious affection and love had brought a rare lump to her throat, but she swallowed it down as she heard someone call out to her.

'Staff Nurse Walker?'

She turned at the sound of her name and there, sitting up in bed, smiling at her in the semi-darkness, was a wonderfully familiar face.

'Miss Tate!'

She went over to the bed, delighted to see her elderly patient from the other day. Her arm was in a sling attached to an IV pole, and she wore a white theatre gown.

'How's your hand doing?' Rachel asked, assuming she had had it repaired.

'The same as when you last saw it.' Miss Tate rolled her eyes. 'My surgery has been cancelled three times. There have been a lot of emergencies. Still, hopefully I'll be sorted this morning. I've been put on "Nil by Mouth" again. It's a good way to go on a diet, let me tell you.'

'You poor thing.'

'Oh, I don't know about that. I'm quite enjoying watching the world go by. What did he do?' She nodded in the direction of Jordan's bed.

'I can't tell you that!' Rachel smiled.

'Well, I heard he was dancing on a table.'

Miss Tate laughed. 'Good for him, I say. I danced on a few tables in my day.'

'Really?'

'Oh, yes.' Miss Tate nodded. 'And I'd dance on them again, given half a chance.'

So would Rachel.

Well, not so much dance on a table, but she felt a growing need to be with Dominic again.

And later, as she came out of Emergency at the end of a very long night shift, Dominic was standing at the entrance.

'Do you want a lift home?' he asked.

'No,' Rachel said.

She went to walk off, but desire was coursing through her, and she could almost taste the lonely regret she would feel if she climbed into her bed alone and missed out on just one more time with him.

Dominic Hadley was her eternal Achilles' heel.

Maybe sleeping with him once more might just clear her head after all—because she was going crazy.

Perhaps in going to bed with him she could

finally put *them* to bed and then move on with her life…?

She knew the arguments were flimsy, but she was too weak to care. She simply wanted to be with him.

And so, instead of walking away, she met his eyes. 'We can go to yours.'

CHAPTER EIGHT

IT WAS RAINING in London.

Just as it had been raining in Sheffield, the sublime second time that they had made love.

'Wait there,' Dominic said. 'I'll bring the car round.'

Rachel stood in the ambulance bay while he dashed through the rain. He had always taken care of those details, Rachel thought. His silver sports car didn't impress her a jot, but the driver certainly did.

He was soaking from his run in the rain. Just as he'd been that time with the stupid golf umbrella when he'd thrown off his parents' warnings about her and made his way to her father's house, Rachel thought as she climbed in.

The wipers swished a little more smoothly than the *thump, thump* of her heart. At a set of traffic lights she turned to look at him, and Dominic turned at the same time, and they smiled their private smile for the first time since they'd met again.

Dominic lived a fifteen-minute drive from the hospital, she found, as the gates opened to a very plush apartment block where they parked in the basement.

They took a lift up to his apartment, but she noticed little about it as she stepped in—just that it was neat and rather large. Because she cared not for the view from the windows…only for the man who took her straight to his bedroom.

He didn't kiss her, and he didn't bother with any preamble. Dominic simply went for the hem of her top and she lifted her arms, compliant and willing.

She wore a rather tired white bra that he deftly removed, and her skin was so pale that you might almost miss the pale pink of her areolae, already gathered and taut at the prospect of his return…

Dominic did not miss them.

Her nipples were awake, and he stroked them with unending fascination, but there was more he wanted to see.

He drew down her trousers and was pleasantly surprised by the tiny silver knickers and the jut of gold beneath.

'God, Rachel,' Dominic said, and paused in the undressing just to stroke and admire.

He slipped his fingers in and felt her for a moment, before stripping off himself. And there, in his bedroom, her mask slipped too.

It always had.

So much so that when he retrieved some condoms from his jacket her nose did that pinched thing, and this time her eyes narrowed too.

'Rachel,' he said. 'I bought these with *you* in mind.'

'Liar.'

'Nope,' he said. 'I lied to myself, but I was always hoping to have you last night—if you'd deigned to show up to the staff do.'

She peeled a condom off with a reluctant smile, for here in his bedroom they could admit to their jealous natures where each other were concerned.

Here, standing naked before him, Rachel could forget her own rules and drop her guard. There was so much desire between them, so much want blazing in their eyes, that she felt safe.

She reached out to touch his body. The strong arms, the broad chest, the toned stomach and the swell of his erection had her trembling with want.

'What's this?' She ran a slender finger over an old white scar, low on his stomach, and watched his muscles jerk tight at her touch.

'I had my appendix out a few—' Dominic started, and then stopped explaining as that same slender finger ran up his thick length.

For Rachel it was like the dessert trolley coming round and having to choose. It was either sink to her knees and taste him, or step towards him and have him inside her.

But he made the choice for her and pulled her in.

Their naked bodies met again, and with the feel of his hard, taut skin against hers, his soft mouth was an exciting contrast. Unlike their kiss in the car park, which had been desperate and urgent, now his mouth was gentle on hers, savouring this reunion.

He had a scent, and a taste, and it was like coming home after a long time away.

His hands were warm on her skin, holding her waist and then moving down and cupping her buttocks, pressing her against him.

Her hand was between them, and he moaned into her mouth as Rachel held him again, strong and velvet beneath her fingers. His kiss roughened as tears stung her eyes at the delight of again being naked and close and intimate with Dominic.

She paused only to slide on the condom, the way they had taught each other so many years ago. Except her hands were shaking even more now than then, as a lick of desire stroked low in her stomach. She thought she might come just from touching him…

His kisses became more demanding, guiding her towards the bed, and they toppled onto it together.

His hand reached between her legs, impatiently parting her willing thighs, both of them desperate for him to be inside her. She guided him greedily, crying out as Dominic seared into her tight oiled space.

They were a knot of limbs and hungry, desperate kisses. He held her face and kissed her cheeks, her lashes, then released her and moved up onto his forearms. It was not a gentle coupling for either of them after all this time, and her legs wrapped tightly around him as he thrust into her.

They had been toying with each other all night—the looks, the food, the pauses, the laughs, the warnings, the nudge of memories… All of it had led them here.

He made the air in the room impossible to breathe. He made the thoughts in her head turn off. He consumed her completely.

And then, when she shattered, when she felt the utter relief of crying out his name as she came, he gave that breathless shout she would crave for ever and released himself into her, collapsing on her in the giddy space they'd made.

Here she was, Rachel thought. The woman she'd lost.

CHAPTER NINE

CERTAINLY IT HAD been a mistake, Rachel thought as she awoke in his arms. A glorious, wonderful mistake that she would remember fondly and never regret. But, yes, it had been a mistake—because now she was right back where she didn't want to be: at the start of the long and painful process of getting over him.

Back to being in love with a man who didn't love her back.

'Hey…' Dominic said as she lifted her head.

'Did it help?' Rachel smiled. 'Did we clear the air?'

'We did,' Dominic said. 'Temporarily at least.'

Because she could tell he already wanted her again, and that he'd been lying there thinking about how right they'd felt. And what that meant.

Rachel was thinking the same.

Here, in his lovely warm bed, their limbs lazy and entwined, it would be so easy to give in to the impossible dream of *them*.

But this had been about sex, Rachel reminded herself.

Although it had always been far more than just that for her.

How did men do it? she wondered. Or rather, how did Dominic separate love from sex so easily?

She didn't seek out gossip, but certainly in the weeks since she'd started at The Primary she'd heard enough to know that Dominic hadn't been lying when he'd said he dated. *A lot.*

It had taken her years to move on and try another relationship—Gordon had seemed ideal, for he had never pushed her out of her comfort zone the way Dominic did. He'd accepted that there were things she simply didn't want to speak about and had left it there—and Rachel had honestly thought she wanted that.

'What are you thinking?'

Rachel laughed to hide her embarrassment—because she could hardly tell him that she'd just been thinking about Gordon!

'It's rude to compare,' Dominic said.

'I wasn't.'

'I should hope not.' He smiled. 'Do you want to know what I was thinking?' he asked.

Rachel wasn't sure that she did.

'I was just thinking about us,' Dominic said as they lay there in the dark. 'If we didn't have a past, and you hadn't been engaged, if we'd met for the first time that morning in Resus, would we be in bed together now?'

'No.' Immediately Rachel shook her head.

'No?' Dominic checked.

'I'd have steered well clear of you,' Rachel said. 'I was warned about you from several sources.'

'I don't believe you.'

But Rachel was insistent. 'If we hadn't already slept together, then I wouldn't be here now. I mean it, Dominic. You're not my type.'

'In what way?'

She lifted one hand from his warm chest and started listing the many ways he did not tick her boxes. 'The reputation, the attitude, the sports car, the vasectomy so you can screw at whim…'

He caught her hand and buried his lips in her palm in a slow, long kiss that she felt all the way down low to her stomach, and when he had made her want him all over again, he refuted what she had said earlier.

'I think we'd be exactly here. In fact, I think we'd have been in bed your first week—possibly even the first night.'

'Oh, no,' she said. 'I take for ever to get into bed.'

'Then *you're* the one who's changed.'

She laughed, a deep low laugh, and it was a forgotten sound that startled her.

Of course there had been laughter in her life since him, but that low belly laugh was one only he had ever elicited—that laugh was private and seductive and it had only ever been heard by Dominic. It was a laugh that provoked, a laugh that begged him to continue this game which always ended in sex.

'I'm telling the truth,' she said.

'Suppose we had just met,' Dominic said.

She wriggled out of his arms and tried

to sit up. But he pulled her back down and pinned her to his chest. Clearly he wanted this conversation and would not let her wriggle out of it.

'Suppose you'd come out for the staff do last night and you'd suspended your morals and we had ended up in bed. We'd be getting to know each other now…'

Rachel was rather sure that she wouldn't like whatever he was scheming, but feigned nonchalance. 'By all accounts, I'd have long since been in a taxi on my way home.'

'I'm not that much of a bastard, Rachel.'

His chest hair was tickling the side of her face and she was focusing on her breathing as she braced herself for his questions.

'So,' he said. 'I would probably be asking are you seeing anyone?'

'Well, I would hope not, given that I'm here…' She cut the rancour and decided to try to play his annoying game. 'No,' she said. 'I've just come out of a long-term relationship.'

'I'm sorry,' Dominic said. 'Do you miss him?' he asked. 'Or her…?'

'Stop it!' Rachel laughed.

'I'm being politically correct, given we don't know each other at all. So,' he asked again, 'do you miss your ex?'

Not as much as I should, Rachel thought as she lay in Dominic's arms. *Not as much as I missed you.*

She settled for, 'It's early days,' and then asked him, 'What about you? Are you seeing anyone?'

'Not really.'

'What sort of answer is that?'

'Okay, no, I'm not seeing anyone seriously.'

'Have you, though?' she asked. 'Have you ever been in a long-term relationship?'

She wanted to fill in the missing years. She loathed that appendix scar—couldn't bear it that he must have lain on an operating table as she went about her day. Her hand moved involuntarily down to cover it.

'No. Well, apart from—'

But Dominic stopped himself from saying *you*, because they weren't supposed to be admitting to the fact that they'd once been married.

He also stopped because her hand was

creeping down his body, so he removed it from the danger zone and caught it again. He was doing his best to tread carefully as he coaxed her out of her shell.

'I think I might need to mend my ways,' he admitted, and was relieved when she gave that low laugh. The one that signalled him to go on.

He didn't quite know what to ask next, because every question led back to them, and so, while he had her warm in his bed, he tried to imagine not knowing the little she'd told him.

He picked up a coil of her thick red hair. 'I love your hair,' he told her. 'Where does it come from?'

He felt her tense even at that simple question.

'My mum,' Rachel said.

'So she's got red hair?'

'Yes,' Rachel said. 'And green eyes like me. She's Irish.' She looked up at him, as if to explain why she was keeping it in the present tense. 'I don't tell all on first dates, Dominic.'

You don't tell all ever, he wanted to bite back, but he did not want to send her hurtling from his bed.

Finally, as they lay silently together, he was rewarded for good behaviour.

'My mum died when I was six.'

'I'm very sorry,' Dominic said carefully, and gave her shoulder a little squeeze. He honestly was. And then he asked what he had asked all those years ago, and awaited her same evasive answer even while hoping for more. 'Do you miss her?'

'Yes,' Rachel said.

'Do you remember her?' he asked, remembering that she'd always said she didn't, really.

'Bits,' Rachel admitted.

And then she allowed him a glimpse of her memories.

'I remember feeling confused when she was teaching me to read. I'd try to follow her finger but I didn't understand how what she was saying could mean "cat". She spun stories,' Rachel explained, and he liked her soft laugh beneath his cheek. 'A short book took for ever for her to read because she would always elaborate and make up new threads.'

They lay in silence and it was she who broke it.

'What about your family?' she asked.

'They're…' *The same*, he was about to say, and then he remembered they were pretending not to know about each other. 'My parents are the poster couple for staying together for the sake of money. They are miserable and it shows,' Dominic said. 'I've barely seen them since…'

It was getting hard for Dominic to play by the rules. Their lives were inextricably linked—a tapestry of a thousand threads, with each stitch linking the next—and it was almost impossible to separate them.

'Do you miss them?' she asked.

'No,' he said. 'In fact, I breathe a huge sigh of relief when the Christmas visit is done with and I don't have to see them again for months.'

'So you only see them at Christmas?'

'And at the odd awards night for my father. I send flowers to my mum on her birthday, and I call her, but again, there's the same breath of relief when I hang up.'

'They must miss having a relationship with you?'

'I don't really know—and to be honest, I don't really care.' He sighed. 'I put myself through medical school, Rachel. They said they wanted to help, but I told them it was way too late for that. It was about then that I stopped trying to look out for everyone else and decided to look out for myself instead. I chose to focus on my career rather than relationships, and while some might call me a bastard, that's only out of hours. I am brilliant at my job.'

'You don't think you can have both?'

'I don't *want* both!' Dominic snapped.

He didn't want to be in lust with his ex-wife, yet clearly he was—given they were wrapped around each other and her hand was back on his appendix scar and all he wanted to do was move it down.

He'd been so certain that he didn't want a relationship with her.

Yet here he lay, not wanting her to leave.

And he'd been so *completely* certain that

he didn't want children that he'd gone and had the snip.

And yet he'd recently checked the success rates of having it reversed.

The rules were falling away, and they could no longer play this game that they were strangers who had only met last night.

Dominic decided that the trouble with bed was… Well, you were naked, and together, and it was all too easy to take one kiss, one deep kiss, and lose yourself in it. Take two, perhaps…

But Dominic would deny them that.

'Rachel…?' He peeled her warm body from him—which was a feat indeed, because he was warm and willing too. 'Why don't I go and get us something to eat?'

It had been a long time since they'd shared her roll in the staff room after all, and perhaps if they could remove all temptation they would be able to speak some more.

As Rachel watched Dominic pull on his trousers and shirt, and retrieve his wallet, his words were still hanging in the air.

'I don't want both.'

He gave her a haphazard kiss on the side of her mouth and tucked his shirt in. 'I won't be long,' he said.

After he'd gone she sat up and hugged her knees.

What the hell was she doing here? Rachel asked herself. What was she doing, playing Dominic's little getting-to-know-you game?

She didn't want her ex-husband to know she was crazy in love with him.

Still.

Still!

What was the point in handing over more of her heart when she knew it was something he didn't want?

She had been lying in her responses right from the start. When he'd asked her if they'd have ended up in bed had they not shared a past, of course the answer had been yes.

Yes, yes, *yes*!

Even if it was thirty years from now that Dominic appeared, even if he hobbled in on a walking stick with grey hair and arthritis, he'd have the ability to throw a hand grenade into her life.

Here was the proof!

Right when her life had finally been put in order, here she was back in Dominic's bed.

But only by chance.

Had she not moved to London and inadvertently taken a job at the hospital where he worked, then she might never have seen him again.

Dominic hadn't sought her out—he hadn't looked her up or tried to get in touch during their thirteen years apart.

It was just sex.

And, while sex with Dominic was bliss, Rachel wanted a relationship that was about more than that. And, as Dominic himself had just clearly stated, he didn't want that.

She wanted more than to warm his bed while he nipped out for a takeaway.

No doubt by Monday they'd be back to attempting to be professional and polite.

And failing.

Rachel knew that if she stayed they'd end up sleeping together again. It was the one thing—the only thing—they could get right.

But this really had to be their last time, because she could not be on call for Dominic and his libido.

Before she left she took out the envelope she'd been carrying in her bag since she'd had the copies of the photographs made and placed it on his dresser, propped up against a bottle of expensive cologne.

And then she wrote a little note and left it on the pillow.

At least now we can remember our last time.

Rachel

They were all caught up now.

Dominic stepped into the bedroom and saw the empty bed and the note on the pillow.

He would never understand her.

Just when they had started talking—*properly* talking—she had withdrawn again.

Just when they had finally been getting somewhere, Rachel had crawled back into her shell.

And then he saw the envelope on the dressing table.

These were the photos he had asked for, and he'd been absolutely right: it hurt to examine the past.

They both looked so young.

So very young that he finally forgave himself for not knowing what the hell to do at the time.

Even now he wasn't sure he would know what to do.

Because there was no such thing as the perfect stillbirth, and no right way to grieve for the loss of a child.

But tonight he was finally starting to.

And as the food went cold, he sat on the edge of his bed and cried for his son.

For the first time he was angry with Rachel.

She should be here, doing this with him.

He had tried so hard with her—he really had. But where was the effort from Rachel?

Had she just handed him this envelope on Friday, he'd have been grateful to look at the photos alone, but she had just left his bed.

Just left his bed and abandoned him to do this alone.

He'd been right all those years ago.

Rachel Walker *was* cold.

CHAPTER TEN

Miss Dorothy Tate
Eighty-two
Tendon repair

DOMINIC'S INTENTION WAS to skim through the notes and then assess the patient for himself—except Rachel's handwriting jumped out at him as if it had been written in neon.

He knew that writing almost as well as he knew his own, and he found that he smiled as he read it. Even her sparse notes said so much about the patient.

Cut hand making soup for the homeless!

He walked into the anaesthetic area and introduced himself. 'How are you, Miss Tate?'

'To be honest, I'm feeling like rather a nuisance.'

'Absolutely you're not,' Dominic refuted.

'Accidents happen. I know your surgery has been cancelled and rescheduled a few times over the weekend, and I'm sorry about that.'

'Well, there have been a lot of emergencies...'

'There have been, but hopefully you've been well looked after?'

'Very much so.' Miss Tate nodded.

Dominic made more small talk as he put in a second IV, in case it was needed. 'What were you doing playing with knives with these hands?' he asked when he saw her gnarled fingers.

'I was making soup.'

'So I read,' Dominic said. 'For the homeless.'

'Well, someone has to take care of them.'

'Yes,' Dominic agreed. 'But how about you let us take care of *you* now?'

He went through the procedure with her and explained that she would be having a regional block rather than a general anaesthetic.

'You won't feel a thing, but I can give you a light sedative if you like.'

'I don't want a sedative. I like to know what's going on. Will you be with me, Doctor?'

'The whole time. So if you change your mind just let me know.'

'I won't change my mind.' Miss Tate smiled.

She watched him as he worked and Dominic could feel her eyes on him.

'You look tired, Doctor,' she said.

'Not at all,' Dominic lied.

'Were you on call last night?'

'No.' He shook his head, and of course he didn't add that he'd been up most of the night looking through photographs.

'You were there on Saturday night,' she commented.

'Where?'

'With Jordan—the one who fell off the table dancing. Such a lovely young man. You stayed by his bed until his wife arrived.'

'Yes.' Dominic nodded.

He went through her medical history. Apart from some arthritis in her hands, there wasn't much of note.

'What's your secret?' he asked.

'I never married,' Miss Tate said, and smiled.

Dominic gave a wry laugh and decided he liked this old girl.

'What about you?' she asked.

He looked down into shrewd bright blue eyes and realised she knew. No doubt she had heard Jordan bringing Heather up to speed—and after he'd asked him not to say anything as well.

Seeing those blue eyes that had seen a whole lot more than he had, Dominic told the truth. 'Once,' he admitted, and saw the eyes of the anaesthetic nurse look up in surprise.

'Married?' the nurse said. 'You?'

'Yep.'

It was a relief to admit it. Dominic was sick of playing by Rachel's rules. Whether she liked it or not, they had once been a couple—a couple who had had a son. He couldn't keep hiding the past, when it was here in front of him, in plain sight.

His past wouldn't be there for much longer, though. Rachel was at this very moment taking herself out of his life.

'Could I have a word, please, May?'

She should have done this the very first day she saw Dominic.

For some people, working alongside an ex might be no big deal. For Rachel, it had proved to be something far worse than hell—it had been a glimpse of impossible bliss.

'I'd really appreciate it if you didn't let on to anyone else that I'm leaving,' she told May. 'I've only been here a few weeks and I'd really rather just slip off.'

And she'd be slipping off very soon, given that she had been here less than a month, which meant there wasn't even any notice to serve. But she agreed to see out the week.

'What about the flat?' May asked. 'Are you going to lose a lot of money for breaking your lease?'

'A bit,' Rachel admitted.

'What price your peace of mind, though?' May smiled. 'We'll be sorry to lose you, Rachel. You're a wonderful emergency nurse. Though I have to say I'm surprised you lasted as long as you did. When you told me you and Gordon had broken up, I expected your notice the next day.'

Gordon.

What a time for May to finally remember his name.

But it was like hearing the name of a song she'd once known—familiar, but the lyrics were a little hard to recall.

Then she took a patient up to the orthopaedic ward, and there, standing at the end of Jordan's bed and having a chat with him, was her song.

Or rather, there was Dominic.

Dominic was the song that made her heart lurch in recall, the song that dragged her up to the dance floor each and every time, the song she sang in the shower, the song she turned up the second she heard the introduction, the song she sang at full volume…

Dominic Hadley was her song.

And she simply had to stop listening to it.

Dominic glanced up and saw her and, still smarting from her walking out on him, turned his back and returned to his conversation with Jordan.

It didn't go unnoticed by Miss Tate, and as he left the ward, she gave him a look.

A look he knew only too well.

A look that told him, *You can behave better than that.*

CHAPTER ELEVEN

HER LAST SHIFT at The Primary.

A late shift.

It was a gorgeous spring day—her first warm one in London—and to celebrate, Rachel had put on a flimsy dress that tied at the side and topped it with a white cardigan and some flat sandals.

She wasn't the only one. Cheered by the first glimpse of sun, everyone seemed to have taken the chance to lose their dark coats and boots. There were people outside the cafés and flowers in pots outside the pub.

It was as if London were pulling out all the stops and trying to persuade her to stay, because she had never seen it so vibrant and pretty.

It was rather a different case at The Primary.

May and a porter were running through the car park with a gurney. Rachel considered going to help, then saw them helping a heavily pregnant woman to stand up and realised it was all under control and she might be needed more inside.

There were ambulances and police cars lined up, and police officers in the corridor when Rachel stepped inside. In fact, the place was so busy that there wasn't even time for a handover.

She went quickly to change into scrubs, then put her hand up for Minor Injuries, where she practically lived now.

Or rather, where she practically hid.

When she went for her coffee break, before the early staff headed off, thankfully there was no Dominic in the staff room.

'Rachel!'

Just as she had on her first day there, she heard May calling her down to the main section.

The timing could not have been worse—because as she walked through the department, she saw Richard and Dominic there.

'I need a word with you before I head off,' May said as she wrote on the whiteboard and then took off her glasses. 'What a day!' She closed her eyes and massaged her temples. 'I have not drawn breath since I got here this morning. That poor woman fainting in the car park…hostage negotiations with a psych patient…'

'Sounds like I missed a bad one.' Rachel pushed out a smile, relieved when she saw that both Dominic and Richard had stood up and were clearly about to leave.

'We're heading back to the ITU, May,' Richard told her.

'But Labour and Delivery are looking for you,' May said.

Richard rolled his eyes. 'We're not covering them.'

'Please, Richard,' May said. 'It's for a patient who was here earlier.'

Richard took the phone with a sigh, and told L&D the same, but then he fell quiet. 'Okay, I'll be right up.'

'I can go.'

'No, no…' Richard said, but then his pager buzzed in his pocket.

Rachel glanced up when he sighed.

'Actually, I have to go to the ITU, so if you could go to L&D? Epidural...'

'Sure,' Dominic said.

'I'll fill you in on the way up.'

This would be the last time she saw Dominic, Rachel thought. Standing there sullen and ignoring her. And she would miss him for ever.

'Poor lass...' May tutted. 'She was going to leave it all to nature, but they must have decided to induce her...'

'Who?' Rachel asked.

May was too busy to answer her, but her words were enough to have Rachel looking at the admission log.

Vanda Callum, aged twenty-seven, was the 'poor lass' who had fainted in the car park.

She'd been in the Emergency Department for all of fifteen minutes, and had soon been transferred to the maternity unit, but there was enough written in the notes for Rachel to know that she had suffered a death in utero.

This type of patient was the very reason that Rachel hadn't been able to face midwifery.

Well, that and the healthy pink babies who cried, too.

How did Dominic do it? Rachel wondered as he and Richard headed off. Because she felt sick inside.

How did he do this? Dominic asked himself as he arrived at Labour and Delivery and Stella, the associate unit manager, handed him the notes.

'Thanks for coming. I know you're not covering us today, but I couldn't get anyone else. Freya's set up for you. Full term,' she said, and went through the history. 'Vanda came up from Antenatal this morning, when they couldn't find a heartbeat. She and her husband decided to go home and have some time there, wait for a natural delivery, but on her way out she fainted in the car park and came back up to us via the ED. She had an ECG and bloods, but it was a simple faint. Just overwhelmed and grieving.'

'Okay,' Dominic said, looking carefully at the heart tracing and blood results as Stella continued to bring him up to speed.

'Dr Mina induced her, and initially Vanda

said she didn't want an epidural, but it's all getting too much for her.'

Dominic nodded.

The Primary was a very busy hospital, with a huge maternity unit, so naturally he had dealt with this sad situation many times, and it was never easy on anyone. But for Dominic, who normally did his level best to keep his memories at bay, today was proving a struggle.

Since seeing those photos, since being with Rachel, it felt new and raw again—as if it had happened only recently.

He slipped quietly into the dark room.

'Here's the anaesthetist now,' Freya said to the patient, with her signature light touch, and she gave Dominic a smile.

Vanda's partner looked up with a grim, helpless and desperate expression that Dominic recognised—for he'd once worn that same expression himself.

'I'm Dominic Hadley, the registrar anaesthetist. What would you prefer me to call you?'

The patient didn't respond.

'Vanda,' her husband said for her. 'And I'm Greg.'

Dominic shook his hand and then explained to Vanda what would be happening. 'I know I can't take the pain of your loss away,' he added. 'But I *can* make you more comfortable.'

He checked all her vitals himself, and then the epidural was quietly done, with Freya holding Vanda as Greg sat with his head in his hands—trying, Dominic guessed, to summon the strength for the next bit.

Rachel hadn't wanted an epidural either.

He remembered standing in a small interview room, with her father and four hulking brothers, trying his eighteen-year-old best to explain to her father what was going on against the background sound of Rachel's pained moans.

'Can't they give her something?' Dave had come close to shouting. 'Can't she have an operation?'

'The doctor says there are risks with surgery.'

'But can't they numb her or something?' Dave had started pacing. 'Can't they give her something to take away her pain? She shouldn't have to go through this. She won't be able to handle it,' Dave had said. 'I'm going to speak to the doctor myself…'

He'd stormed off and Dominic had gone after him, desperate to avoid her father bursting into the delivery suite and causing a scene.

'Dave, I really think we should listen to Rachel…'

'What would *you* know? This is all your bloody fault!' Dave had flung at him.

And then he'd given Dominic a look—*such* a look—for all the ways he had made his daughter suffer.

Dominic had forced himself to speak. 'Dave… Can we put things aside for tonight, please? Just keep it down for Rachel's sake? She needs us to be calm.'

'You don't get it. It's going to be like when her mum died all over again. She was inconsolable, Dominic…'

Dave had pressed his fingers into his eyes and Dominic had stood there, not knowing what to say because he simply hadn't known this side of Rachel.

'We were all upset—of course we were,' Dave had continued. 'I was devastated. But

Rachel was terrible. Every night she cried herself to sleep, and then woke up crying the next day. I had to fetch her out of school more times than I can count.'

'I didn't know that,' Dominic had admitted. 'But, Dave, I can only go on what she's telling me now. And she's telling me and the midwife and the doctor that she doesn't want anything for the pain…'

Dave had started to cry then—only the second time he'd seen Rachel's father's tears. The first time had been when Dominic had told him his daughter was pregnant and Dave had said he wished her mother was here. He'd said the same thing again.

'I wish her mother was here. She'd know what to do.' And then he'd wiped his eyes and blown his nose and taken a big breath. 'Tears aren't going to get us anywhere. You're right, lad. We have to listen to Rachel. We both want what's best for her.'

'We do,' Dominic had said, relieved that her father wasn't going to make a scene. 'I'd better go back in.'

He did not want to relive that night.

But he was doing it—he was—and he

ached for this young couple and their journey ahead.

'There you go,' Dominic said as he secured the epidural. 'It's all done. It will start to take effect very soon.'

He helped Freya get Vanda lying back in the bed, and then slipped away to write up his notes.

A short while later Freya joined him. 'Thanks for that.'

'No problem.'

'I'm just giving them some space,' Freya said, and then sighed as she sat down. 'I've got the best job in the world most of the time, but nights like this kind of redress the balance.'

Dominic made no comment. He was in absolutely no mood for a chat.

Freya looked over to him. 'You were ever so nice to her.'

'I would hope so,' Dominic clipped.

He did *not* want to talk about this, so he quickly concluded his notes. But as he headed off, he ran into Richard coming out of the lift.

'Everything okay?' he asked.

'Yep.' Dominic nodded. 'Freya's at the desk.'

'I'm not looking for Freya—I came to check on you.'

'Why?'

'Because I saw your ex-wife's face when she looked at the admissions log. Because there's an obvious reason why teenagers might feel they have to get married. And because, assuming you don't have a teenager of your own that you haven't told me about, this patient will have been difficult for you. Freya and I—'

'Oh, for God's sake!' Dominic retorted. So that attempt at a chat from Freya had been for *his* benefit. 'Leave it, Richard,' Dominic warned him—except the muscles in his jaw knitted and he was appalled to feel that he might break down in the hospital corridor.

He strode off, cross with Richard for discussing it with Freya, but all the while knowing he would have done the same had the situation been the other way around.

He didn't need them meddling in his love life.

Love life?

What a joke.

He leant against the wall and closed his eyes.

He'd hurt Rachel so badly, and taken away the chance of the one thing she wanted most. They'd been over before they'd even started. They couldn't even speak about their son…

Or rather, Rachel wouldn't.

Nor would she speak about the end of their marriage.

And neither would she speak about her mum.

Yet she'd been inconsolable when she'd died—Dave had told him as much. Or rather, Dave had said she'd been *terrible.*

He thought of his own stunned reaction to the matter-of-fact way she'd spoken about her mother all those years ago, then pressed his knuckles into his mouth when he thought of Dave Walker and his brusque, insensitive ways dealing with a grieving six-year-old child.

Rachel wasn't cold. Dominic knew that then. The poor thing was frozen.

And he couldn't blame Dave, because he didn't know how to talk about it either—

especially with Rachel. There was so much other stuff that got in the way…

And then he looked back to the L&D unit and thought about the couple in there, and he hoped that they'd do better than he and Rachel had.

They had to speak about Christopher. But it always got mired in other stuff—their marriage, their break-up, their families…

Dominic took a breath, and summoned those nerves of steel he'd fought to acquire.

At work he could shut out the world and focus only on the task.

And that was exactly what he needed to do now.

'See you, Rachel!' Tara said.

Probably not, Rachel thought, but smiled and gave a little wave as Tara headed off.

And that was that.

She'd said goodbye to May when she'd finished at four—that had been the reason May had called her down—but apart from May, no one knew her time at The Primary was done.

What on earth had she been thinking to

wear a flimsy dress when it was only March? she wondered. Because that lovely warm spring day had turned into a blowy cold night when she stepped out into the draughty corridor.

And there waiting for her was Dominic.

'Rachel,' said Dominic, and pushed off from the wall he'd been leaning on.

'Oh, did we agree to have sex again?'

Rachel was at her sarcastic best.

'Only, I must have forgotten to pencil you in.'

'No.' Dominic couldn't help but smile as she sniped at him. 'I came here so we could talk.'

'Well, I don't want to talk to you,' Rachel said.

'I know you don't,' Dominic said. 'You've made that abundantly clear.' He called out to her departing back. 'You're walking off now just as you walked out on us the other night—just as you walked out on our marriage.'

She turned furiously to him. 'I did not walk out on our marriage.'

'You withdrew,' Dominic said, but then he caught himself—because he had not come down here to row about their marriage, nor about the other night.

Focus on the reason you're here, Dominic reminded himself.

'I came down to ask if we can speak about Christopher.'

'You're at work, Dominic.'

'I've asked a colleague to cover me for as long as it takes, and Richard's loaned me his office so we won't be disturbed.'

He didn't want to do this at work, but neither did he want this conversation to take place in a bar or restaurant. And as for his home—well, there was the distraction of a bed.

And he and Rachel did *not* need the distraction of a bed.

Here at work he could focus better, and right now he was entirely focused on *her*. On the jut of her chin, the glare in her eyes that warned him to stay back.

Well, no more.

'I don't want to talk about it,' she said.

'Why?' Dominic persisted, refusing to back off.

He saw her blinking rapidly.

'Why can't we talk about it?'

Rachel could feel the flutter of her pulse in her throat and her eyes darted to the entrance as she planned a swift exit.

'He was our son and I think it's time we spoke about him together, but you have to want to,' said Dominic.

She'd *always* wanted to, but she was terrified of breaking down, scared of showing the depth of her pain.

'I might get upset,' she said.

'Yes,' Dominic agreed, looking at her.

To the rest of the world they might look as if they were discussing the weather, but she knew there was so much more if only she could let him in.

'You probably will get upset, and no doubt so will I.'

She looked at him, standing so steady and together and strong.

'I can take your pain, Rachel,' he said. 'If you'll let me.'

'What if you can't?' Her voice was hoarse with strain.

'Rachel, I *can*.'

He sounded so certain that it steadied the panic that clawed at her throat.

She knew this was her last chance to speak of Christopher with him, given she was leaving, but more than that, after Dominic's admission that he too might get upset, she finally felt ready.

'Come on,' he said.

They walked together up the long corridor, not touching, but then she shivered, and he must have seen her, and not caring that someone might see, nor what they might think, he put an arm around her and held her hand.

She was grateful for his warmth.

He put on the *Do Not Disturb* light outside Richard's door and, barring all hell breaking loose in ED, for now it was just the two of them.

There was a picture on Richard's desk, of him with Freya and their baby, and her eyes were drawn to that because she wanted that happy family photo so badly.

Instead of the one she had tucked inside that folder.

'Thanks for the photos,' Dominic said. 'Though not...'

He'd been about to say, *Not for the way you left them*, she thought, but stopped himself.

'It's good to finally have them.'

'I should have sent them to you years ago,' Rachel admitted. 'Although I didn't know where. Still, I should have tried...'

'Rachel, I wasn't ready to look at them...' Dominic paused. 'Until the other night.'

He took out his wallet and opened it up, and then positioned it so that a picture of the three of them now sat on the desk. She gazed on the photo for a long moment and then looked at Dominic, at his pale face and lips and the shadows under his eyes, and then she blinked in surprise when he gave her a slow smile.

'He was beautiful.'

She nodded.

'He had your hands,' Dominic said, and he took her hand and examined it, as if confirming that his memory was correct as he held her long fingers. 'I remember holding him and thinking I'd never seen such perfect hands apart from yours.'

He had been too delicate to be held for very long, but there had been those treasured cuddles, and she shared one of her memories now.

'He had your mouth.'

Beautiful lips that she had wanted so desperately to see stretch and cry and one day smile if only he'd had the chance…

'Why couldn't he have lived?' she asked.

'I don't know.'

'Why?' She asked the impossible question again. 'I feel like everything died that day.' She started to cry—not loudly, but tears were beginning to spill out. 'Not just Christopher, but us, and everything I ever wanted to be, all just died with him.'

'I know.'

Rachel really cried then, and for the first time since her mum had died, she wasn't reprimanded for it. Or told to *'Hush'*, or *'Enough now'*, or be taken to the park.

Dominic moved his chair close to hers and held her and let her cry.

'His legs…' Rachel said, and Dominic crumpled, when he thought of those sturdy little legs that had never kicked, never walked, never run.

He wanted the quiet glory of running with his son.

That feeling when you knew you had just conquered the world.

He should have seen his son shoot out of the starting blocks and on to victory. His legs, even in the bewilderment of death, had been present and strong.

When Rachel looked up and saw that Dominic was crying too, she didn't know how to react. There were tears on his cheeks and in his velvet brown eyes. She'd never seen him like this in her life, and somehow it helped to see him cry for their little son.

'There was nothing I could do for him,' Dominic rasped. 'Nothing. I couldn't even warm him.'

She remembered Dominic tucking a blanket around him and holding him close, and that made her cry all over again, but it felt better to cry with him, to witness his love and to share their grief together.

'I wanted him back inside me, alive and growing,' she said. 'It was like when Mum died.'

She had never told him that, but had always wanted to, and they weren't going off track now—they were finally on it.

'What was it like?' he asked.

'I just wanted it all to go back to how it was, but everything had changed.' She felt as if she were choking. 'Then everything did go back to how it had been—everything just carried on except *without* her. I don't even know if they miss her…'

'Of course they do. Rachel, it's just the way your dad is, but I know for a fact he misses her. The night we lost Christopher he cried, and said he wished your mum was there.'

'Dad cried?'

'Yes—and he cried and said exactly the same thing to me on the night I told him you were pregnant.'

She'd never known what had been said that night—just that Dominic had come to the pub and said they would marry.

'Your dad loved your mum, just as he would have loved Christopher. And you know that. You *do* know that. It's just his way, Rachel.'

'But everyone said he was a mistake.'

'Yes,' Dominic said, 'and even I thought the same at first. But once I got used to the idea—well, he stopped being a mistake, didn't he? We *both* wanted him.'

They had—they really had.

'I'm not going to hide him any more,' Dominic said, and she looked up at his words. 'I don't have a child but I *did* have a son—and he changed me and the direction of my life. I'm a doctor because of him.'

And that made her cry all over again, because it was something so tangible in a sea of what-ifs, and something good to come out of so much grief.

'There's always going to be a part of me missing, but, Rachel—'

Dominic cut himself off and dragged in a breath, reminding himself not to cloud this conversation. This was about Christopher and what he had brought to their lives. The rest they could deal with in the fullness of time.

And, while he wanted to ask her when they could speak again, when they could talk about *them*, he did not want to push too hard too soon.

And so, rather than talk about trying again, and vasectomies and things, and the terror of doing it all over again, he moved back to their little lost son.

'He was wanted and loved.'

And now that Rachel had taken off those thorn-rimmed glasses, shaded with resentment and pain, she could recall softer, kinder times—Dominic coming home after a long shift at the bar and crawling into bed exhausted, holding both her and the bump of their baby as she slept in his arms.

She spoke to him about the little pair of socks that she'd kept. Remembering how he'd come home with them one evening because they were cute.

And together they recalled the two of them cuddled up under blankets on the sofa, because they were saving to feed the electricity meter when their baby was born, and the flat would need to be kept warm.

It was nice to remember all this, but also terribly hard to do so. And so, when they were all wrung out, she closed up his wallet and handed it to him and watched him slip it back into his jacket. It was nice to know the photo now lived by his heart.

'You know,' she said as she peeled some tissues from the box, 'despite the tears, I do feel better.'

'Good,' Dominic said, and took a couple of tissues for himself.

'Will you be all right to work?' she asked.

He nodded. 'I'll get you a taxi home.'

'Don't be daft,' Rachel said, and she looked at him, this man who might not love her but who had always taken care of her. 'I'll be fine. Thanks for this,' she said, and she meant it.

Because talking about her son, being able to share her memories of Christopher Hadley with his father…

It had meant the world.

CHAPTER TWELVE

'WHO ARE YOU here to see, Dominic?' May was updating the whiteboard. 'The surgeons are—'

'I'm actually here to see Rachel,' Dominic cut in.

He had given her a few days' space, so as not to cloud their conversation about Christopher with the other issues surrounding their relationship, but he could no longer hold back.

Now Dominic *wanted* to cloud the issue. It was time. They belonged together. There could be no doubt.

'Rachel Walker,' he elaborated when May frowned.

'But Rachel's not here.'

'When's she back on?'

'She's not,' May said, and carried on writing on the whiteboard. 'Rachel left last week.'

'What do you mean, she left?'

'Just that.'

May wasn't exactly forthcoming.

'It was supposed to be a three-month trial, but it wasn't working out, so she left before the end of it and headed back to Sheffield.'

'May, I really need to speak to her. Can you give me her mobile phone number?'

'I'm not about to give you one of my nurses' contact details.' May gave him a rather scornful look. 'I'm not the keeper of your little black book, Dominic. It would be a full-time job, that's for sure.'

'May…' Dominic was appalled that Rachel had gone and was way past caring about keeping secrets. 'Rachel is my ex-wife.'

'Jesus, Mary and Joseph!' May put down the whiteboard marker. 'Are you sure?'

'I think I'd know.'

'But you never let on.'

'Rachel didn't want me to,' Dominic said. 'Anyway, it was years ago.'

'Yet you're standing here asking for her number.'

'Because I *have* to speak to her.'

May was kinder then, but still adamant.

'Dominic, I won't be giving you her phone number. If she'd wanted you to have it you would have it.'

Rachel exited the train station at Sheffield and returned to her life without Dominic.

There was blossom on the trees, and everything looked gorgeous and green as the taxi carried her back to her dad's. She wore the same summery dress she'd had on when she'd last seen Dominic, but despite the attire, and the familiar sights of home, tears kept stinging her eyes and she wondered what on earth she'd done.

Since that night, talking with Dominic, she'd been like a leaking tap—only her tears weren't all about Christopher.

He'd told her in bed that morning that he wanted to work rather than to have a relationship. He'd outright said that he didn't want both. And even at their most intimate, holding each other and crying about their son, Dominic hadn't wanted to talk about *them*.

She had to accept it. Because she could not go through it again and again.

Rachel felt like a failure as she paid the

taxi driver and hauled out her case. She was thirty-two years old and moving back in with her dad. Well, just for a couple of weeks, until she found somewhere of her own.

As she walked up the garden path she saw the front door open.

'Dad!' She barely recognised him. His beard was gone, his scruffy grey hair was freshly cut, and he was wearing, of all things—

'What are you doing in a *lilac* jumper?'

'It's blue,' her dad insisted.

'It isn't,' Rachel said as she hugged him, and then pulled back when she saw his lady friend coming out of the kitchen. 'Oh, hi, Moira,' she said, when what she really wanted to ask was, *What have you done to my dad?*

Rachel did not want to be back living at her dad's. And now she couldn't even hide herself away in the kitchen, as Moira seemed to have that under control.

'Dinner won't be long,' Moira said as Rachel took a seat in the very tidy lounge on a sofa that had new cushions.

Clearly it wasn't just her dad that Moira was sprucing up!

Moira lived here, Rachel realised. Or if she didn't quite live here fully yet, she soon would.

For dinner they were no longer formally seated at the dining table, but squashed on the sofa in the lounge, eating spaghetti bolognaise from trays on their laps.

And when they'd finished eating it was Moira who went to take the plates.

'I'll do it,' her dad said, and stood up, no doubt to micro-manage the stacking of the dishwasher.

'Sit down, Dave,' Moira said. '*I'll* do it.'

And when her dad sat down, and allowed someone else to stack his precious dishwasher, Rachel knew just how serious the two of them were. On top of that, he patted Moira's bottom as she walked past.

Oh, God—Rachel could not bear the thought of them in bed together!

'I'll probably stay at Nicola's,' Rachel said, mentioning a friend oh, so casually. 'I'll just borrow my old room for a couple of nights.'

'No rush,' Dave said as Moira came back in.

And as they watched a replay of a dancing

show on TV, Rachel found out that he and Moira were thinking of taking up ballroom dancing!

The whole world was moving on and having relationships and falling in love and having babies. All except for her.

Rachel could feel the sting of tears at the back of her eyes.

'Our Phil's dropping in,' Dave said during the adverts. 'He's bringing over the gender-reveal cake, but he's taping it up so we can't peek. We're going to have a little party here.'

How did her dad even know what a gender-reveal cake *was*? Things really were changing here…

But she knew her dad loved nothing more than a little party, with all the family present, so Rachel pushed out a smile. 'When?'

'Tomorrow. If it's a boy, it's going to be called Robin, but if it's a girl—'

'Don't start, Dave…' Moira sighed.

'Pixie!' her dad said, in the most scathing of tones. 'I've lived too long—I really have. Eleven grandchildren and one of them called *Pixie*!'

'You have twelve grandchildren,' Rachel said, her voice shaking.

It was only the fact that she now knew her dad had cried about Christopher that made her brave enough to raise it.

'You have twelve—but, oh, that's right… We don't speak about Christopher.'

'Because I don't want to upset you.'

'Has seeing Dominic stirred things up?' Moira asked.

Rachel pursed her lips at the intrusive question. Clearly Moira had been told all about it. But even as she did that, tears were trickling down her face, and there was nowhere to go, nowhere to hide except her old bedroom, and somehow the thought of that just made things worse.

'Come on, love,' Dad said. 'Don't go upsetting yourself.'

'I think you need to tell her, Dave,' Moira said.

'Moira!' he warned.

Rachel looked up. 'Tell me what?'

'It's nothing,' he said. 'It was years ago.'

But Moira was insistent. 'She still needs to know.'

'Very well,' Dave said. 'Dominic called me.'

'When?' Rachel asked, and her heart soared with hope.

But of course it was a false alarm.

'A couple of years after you broke up.'

'Oh.' She sagged back in the seat.

'You know how he insisted that he'd pay me back for…' He swallowed. 'For Christopher's funeral. I always said there was no need. I was more than glad to take the strain off the two of you…'

Somewhere in the recesses of her mind, lost in that appalling time, there was a memory of that. Her dad saying he would take care of things and Dominic swallowing his pride, insisting it was to be just a loan.

'When?' Rachel croaked. 'When did he pay you back?'

'He'd send some money every month until he'd paid me back. It was just something he felt he had to do. I didn't want to go worrying you with talk about it.'

It made her feel very small to realise that her assumption that Dominic had walked off without a backward glance could not be further from the truth. He had told her that he'd put himself through med school, and now she was finding out that on top of that he'd been paying her dad back—doing what little he had been able for their son.

'He called to thank me for the loan and he wanted to know how you were…said that he was studying to be a doctor…'

'What else did he say?'

'Nothing much.' Her dad shrugged. 'He just wanted to know how you were.'

'Dave!' Moira said again. 'Tell her about the other time. Two years ago.'

Rachel turned and looked at her father, and despite the new jumper and the fresh haircut, she could see the strain on his features, and she noticed that he was clinging on to Moira's hand.

'Your dad told me a few things after you were here the last time. Well, I dragged it out of him,' said Moira.

'What?'

'I think he'd been drinking,' said her dad.

'Dominic?' Rachel frowned, because Dominic didn't drink—well, not much—but it would seem that one night two years ago he had.

'It was his thirtieth birthday and he was all mawkish. Said he wanted to get in touch and find out for himself how you were. He wanted your phone number.'

'And?' Rachel said.

'He said he'd tried to find you on social media and the like.'

'What did you say?'

'That perhaps there was a reason you didn't want to be found,' her dad said. 'I told him you had started seeing someone… Gordon. That you were back on track and for the first time in years you actually seemed happy. I said that if he cared about you—if he really cared about you—then it would be better for all concerned for him to leave well alone.'

Rachel hadn't known it was possible to feel so cross, and yet so relieved, so bewildered, and yet so clear-headed, all at the same time. Dominic—arrogant, confident, alley cat Dominic—had struggled too.

'Why the hell didn't you tell me?'

'Because I didn't want to bring up old hurts,' her dad snapped. 'That man caused you no end of problems…'

'I loved *that man*, though,' Rachel choked.

The doorbell went. No doubt it was Phil with the cake.

Her dad, glad of the reprieve, jumped up to get it while Rachel sat silent, with tears coursing down her cheeks.

'He meant well,' Moira said. 'It's been eating him up.'

'I know he meant well.' Rachel felt her anger towards her father fading. He'd been the one who'd had to deal with the fallout of their divorce after all, and she could understand his desire to protect her.

'I'm sorry for your loss, Rachel,' Moira said.

'Thank you,' Rachel responded politely, and then tried to pull back from discussing it further with Moira. 'It was years ago, though…'

'And tidied up and put away still festering.'

'Yes,' Rachel said, and she looked over at Moira with less wary eyes.

Dominic had been right. She must be pretty special to have got all that information out of her dad.

Rachel was starting to see how much she had lost by keeping her distance from people, and as her father helped Phil in with the cake, she relaxed and opened up to Moira.

'Does it change things?' Moira asked. 'Knowing that he called?'

'A bit,' Rachel admitted. 'Although I know he was trying to get hold of photos and things. Still, it helps to know that he paid for the funeral.'

They watched the dancers on TV for a moment, but then Rachel had a question for Moira.

'How did you get Dad to tell you?'

'I asked him,' Moira said. 'After that dinner we had I knew there was something bothering him, but when I asked what it was he said it was none of my business.'

'What did *you* say?'

'I didn't say anything. I went and got my coat,' Moira said. 'And when he asked why I was huffing off, I told him that if he wanted me in his life, then it most certainly *was* my business. That I'm not going to be fobbed off.'

And apparently there was someone else who refused to be fobbed off.

'Er… Rachel…' Her dad stood at the living

room door, his face bright red and clashing with his lilac jumper. 'You've got a visitor.'

And there behind him stood Dominic.

He did not stand quietly, for there was such a presence to him, dressed in black jeans and a black jumper, unshaven and pale.

She couldn't take her eyes off him.

'Dominic.' Moira stood and introduced herself. 'I'm Moira—a friend of Dave's.'

'It's nice to meet you, Moira.'

Rachel watched as Dominic walked in and shook Moira's hand. It was all so terribly polite and so very odd to have Dominic Hadley back in the Walker living room.

It was more than odd for Dominic. There was the strangest feeling of déjà vu as he stood at the fireplace where he all those years ago had told Dave Walker that he'd got his daughter pregnant.

He'd been terrified then, but he wasn't terrified now—because he was here to finally put things right.

'I'm sorry to mess up your evening,' Dominic said to the one friendly face in the room.

'No, no,' said Moira, 'it's no bother. We

were just watching the television.' She glanced over to Rachel, whose skin was bright red, her eyes all puffy and glassy from crying. 'And having something to eat…' she added rather lamely.

'Rachel.' Dominic turned to her then. 'I was hoping that we might speak.'

She nodded—what else could she do?

'Perhaps we could go for a walk?'

'Sure.' She pulled herself up from the chair and gave a thin smile to her worried-looking dad.

'Take care,' Dave said, and his voice was gruff.

Dominic could feel his reluctance to let her leave, but he stepped back and allowed the two of them to pass.

Rachel couldn't quite believe he was here. Her head was still whirring from the fact that he had called her dad. Twice. That the man she'd thought had walked away without a backward glance had spent two years sending money to her father.

That was the Dominic she had known—the man she had loved from the start.

'He's watching us from the window,' Dominic said as they walked. 'I can *feel* it.'

'I know…' Rachel sighed. 'He means well.'

'He does,' Dominic said. 'He's a good guy.'

She gave a mocking laugh, because she knew the two men she loved did not get on.

'He really is,' Dominic said. 'I can't imagine losing the woman I love and then having to run my own business as well as raise five kids.'

'Nor can I,' Rachel admitted.

'And then, just when he'd got them almost done—just when the youngest was close to finishing school—along came some guy and got her pregnant.'

Her cheeks were sore from the tears that were still trickling down as they walked familiar streets, passing their old school and the tree where they had shared her roll on the first day of the school year—where she'd smiled her metallic NHS braces smile at Dominic Hadley as she'd handed over her heart.

Because she had fallen in love at first sight.

And love could be so hard.

Impossible, even, when you were told it

was just a crush, that you were too young, and your feelings would fade.

They paused a moment at the school gates, where she'd stood waiting for him to finish his exams so she could tell him about the baby, and she remembered watching his smile fade.

'Come on,' he said, and they walked on past the school and towards the park.

'Why did you leave without saying goodbye?' Dominic asked quietly.

'Because we'd said all we had to say.'

'Had we?' Dominic checked. 'Because there are an awful lot of things I want to say to you that I haven't, and I've always felt you've been holding back.'

'That's right. I'm cold.'

'You're not, though,' Dominic said. 'Are you?'

'No.'

They arrived at the park—the same park where her brothers had swung her and bounced her, so she'd return home with a smile rather than admit to her pain. The same park where she'd lain on the grass next to

Dominic and told herself she could never have him.

There were so many hurts, but there was one in particular that still festered beneath all the others that were beginning to heal.

'I loved you,' she told him, without looking at him.

'Yet you never once told me that.'

'Because I was scared to,' Rachel admitted. 'Because I loved you and you didn't love me.'

'You don't know that.'

'But I *did* know that,' Rachel said, and turned to face him. 'I loved you the day I met you and I had to hold back from telling you over and over. I would have married you baby or no baby—would you really have wanted to hear that?'

He was silent.

'The day we got married I wanted to come to this park and spin and dance like I was Maria in *The Sound of Music*. I wanted to cry because I was so happy. Yet there was a part of me that knew you'd only married me because of the baby.'

'Perhaps, but—'

'No buts,' Rachel said. 'Please don't lie to

me here, Dominic. You married me because I was pregnant. I knew it, you knew it, and everyone else knew it too. And so, yes, I held back. I was so happy, but I felt guilty for being happy, so I tried to hold back, because I didn't want to smother you. I didn't want to be hanging-off-the-lampposts happy when the truth was we were only together because of the baby.'

'No,' he said. 'We were together first.'

'You didn't love me, Dominic. At least not the way I loved you.'

Rachel felt oddly relieved. The truth was out and there was nothing to hide any more.

Dominic opened his mouth to speak and then closed it. Because her revelation had been unexpected. Because he'd thought he might have to coax an admission of love from Rachel.

Now he faced the force of it, as they sat on the bench in silence and looked out at the park.

Dominic needed to think about this—not just dismiss her deepest thoughts, or sugar-coat things just to whitewash their history—and he took a moment to consider.

She was right, and she was wrong, and she was all shades of everything in between.

'You say you loved me, Rachel, but you never trusted me. I know you were grieving and depressed after we lost Christopher, and I'm sorry for my handling of that, but you pushed me away right from the very start.'

'No—'

'Yes,' he said firmly. He stated it calmly and as fact. 'You never let me in. Even when I asked about your mother…'

'You didn't want to hear all that.'

'Of course I did,' Dominic refuted. 'I didn't expect you to open up the day you first told me, but even over the weeks, over the months, over the years, you never gave me the parts of you that mattered the most.'

He said it not as a criticism—in fact, he held her hand.

'I get it, Rachel. I didn't then, but I do now. You were shut down by your family. But as for me not loving you…'

He was trying to be logical, but he was also bewildered.

'I didn't know what love was back then, Rachel,' he admitted. 'And I'm not making excuses—it's the truth. My parents told me they loved me in the same breath as they told me all the things they did for me. But that didn't feel much like love. And then everyone told me I'd ruined both our lives and that we'd never make anything of ourselves, and that didn't sound a lot like love.'

Rachel turned and looked at him.

'I know that I wanted to look after you, and that I failed to do so.'

'It wasn't your fault.'

'It felt as if it was at the time,' Dominic said. 'You say I didn't fight for us—but I tried. I even offered to move in with your dad! And when you said it was time to put it all behind us, to move on with our lives, that all we'd done was make each other unhappy, I believed you meant what you said. You know how I felt about my mother staying with my father. I would never have wanted to keep you in an unhappy marriage.'

'I overheard your dad talking to you,' she admitted.

'He never spoke *for* me. Those were *his*

words—never mine. I've barely spoken to him since that day. Why didn't you just ask me what I wanted? How I felt?'

'Because I was scared to,' Rachel admitted. 'Because I knew how much I loved you and I didn't want to hear that you didn't love me.'

'And do you still?'

'Still what?'

'Rachel!'

'Do I still love you?'

Rachel looked at his velvet brown eyes and she was simply too tired to deny, deny, deny. It was finally time to be honest, no matter what the consequences.

'Yes, Dominic, I do.'

'Then what were you doing walking out on me the other day? You left me with those photos, Rachel, and that hurt.'

'You'd just told me you didn't want both a relationship *and* work,' she reminded him, 'and then you headed out to get takeaway.'

'We were *talking*, Rachel. For the first time in years we were properly talking... Okay, maybe it wasn't the best time to pause the conversation, but I was trying to get us out of bed and actually speak. Because if you love me…'

'I *do* love you.'

'Even if I can't give you babies?'

'Of course I still love you.'

Oh, she wanted a baby, wanted a family, but the love she felt was independent of that.

'You *get* me.'

'When you let me.' Dominic smiled.

'I'm sorry I'm not good at sharing my feelings.'

She decided to try hard and let him know some of the things that made her love him so.

'I love how you hold my hand, even when we row.'

It was one of the nicest of things he did. Even during difficult conversations he was still holding her and looking out for her.

'And I love how you make me smile, even when I'm trying not to, and I love your terrible attempts at a northern accent. I love how you're so patient with my dad, and how you paid him back…'

She saw the press of Dominic's lips, as if it was he who was having to work hard to hold his feelings in now.

'That means everything to me. And I also love that you called him twice...'

'He told you?' Dominic closed his eyes, looking both embarrassed and relieved that her father had told her.

'Was it about the photos?' she asked.

'In part,' Dominic said, and then stood. 'Come on.'

'Where?'

'It's just easier to do this while we're walking.'

He was nervous, Rachel realised, and that was so unlike the Dominic she now knew.

He cleared his throat. 'After I'd paid him back, I had a letter from your dad. I've still got it,' he admitted as they left the park. 'He said that we were square, and he wished me all the best. But I didn't want it to be over, Rachel, and I just had to know if you were okay. When I called, your dad said you were getting there, and that me getting in touch would only make things worse. I couldn't argue with that.'

They turned in to the street where they had once lived, and she smiled when she saw the little flat they had shared.

'And the second time?'

'It was my thirtieth. I don't usually drink, but I went out with Jordan and he told me Heather was expecting. I don't know… It just got too much. I told him about Christopher and you, and I realised I'd never come close to finding what I'd once found with you. I missed what we'd once had. You say that I didn't love you, but looking back, I know I did—I just didn't know it at the time. That night we had the curry…'

She blushed at the memory.

'I was in love with you then, Rachel, and I love you now. I've never stopped loving you.'

She looked up into his eyes, and felt his hands on her cheeks, his fingers wiping away her tears. 'Please don't just say it.'

'Why would I just say it? If I didn't want us to be together, why would I have got in my car this morning and driven all the way up here to put us through this? Why have I been finding out about vasectomy reversals…?'

'Stop it.'

'But I have been,' Dominic said.

'Since you looked at the photos?'

'No, since we had that awful lunch in the

canteen.' He smiled at her frown. 'I was absolutely certain when I had it—right up to when you came to The Primary. But I'm not so certain now. I don't want to take away our chances.'

Finally, after all this time, she dared to say what she had wanted to for so very long. 'Can we try again?'

'We'll do more than try,' Dominic told her. 'I love you, Rachel Walker, and I'm going to spend the rest of my life proving that to you. Come on,' he said again.

'Where?' Rachel frowned as she was trotted off again.

'Here.'

She frowned again as he reached into his jeans and took out a key, opened the door. 'What are you doing?'

'I didn't come straight to your father's when I arrived in Sheffield,' Dominic said. 'And I didn't fancy a hotel, nor having to show up at your father's door whenever I wanted to see you. I decided we'd done enough of that and I went to speak to our old landlord. The flat is ours for the next two weeks. I figured that might give us time to work things out. I didn't know you'd be so easy to convince…'

She was stunned, but smiling, and a little overwhelmed to be walking through this door again.

And then Dominic picked her up and carried her—as he *hadn't* done on their wedding night.

Yes, she liked this rather more arrogant version of him. And there was another new side to him too…

He put her down in the little lounge, where there were fresh-cut flowers in a vase on the table.

'You've been shopping,' she said.

'There's food in the cupboards,' Dominic said as she peered into the kitchen, 'and I've made us roast pumpkin soup.'

'Seriously?'

'I got the recipe from a patient. Chilli flakes are the secret ingredient to a good soup, you know.'

'I *do* know.' Rachel smiled. 'But how do you?'

'It was a *very* lengthy tendon repair.' Dominic smiled. 'Miss Tate could teach us all a thing or three...'

Miss Tate had chatted not only about soup, but also about the importance of flowers, and being kind—all the things he hadn't learnt from his parents. And then she'd told him how, if she had her time again, she would take more chances and maybe not hold back on love.

They hadn't been talking about Dominic, yet he'd felt a little as if they had. And it had been a pleasure to sit on his stool beside such a wonderful lady.

'Dominic, it all looks gorgeous,' Rachel said.

There were flowers on the little table too, where once there had been doctor's letters and bills.

'What time did you get here?'

'I went to see May this morning, around eight, and left pretty soon after that. Richard has said he doesn't want me back until this is sorted. Although I was prepared for quite a lengthy negotiation.'

He led her to the bedroom, which had the

same brown walls and grotty curtains, the same heavy wooden bed, but…

'New sheets?' She smiled.

'New everything,' Dominic said, and then he pulled her to him. 'A brand-new start. Rachel, will you please marry me?' he asked, and then added, 'Again?'

'You mean it?'

'I have never been more certain of anything in my life,' he said. 'In fact, I've still got my wedding ring.'

'So have I!' Rachel laughed.

'And this time you're getting an engagement ring.'

'I don't need one.'

'Well, you're getting one,' Dominic said. 'This time we're doing it right, and that starts tonight. I've already told your dad I'm asking you to marry me.'

'When?' Rachel frowned.

'When he came to the door. He was about to send me away until I pointed out that that hadn't worked in the past. I said that if you didn't want me in your life, then I had to hear it from you. I said I loved you, and that

I was going to do whatever I could to make things better.'

'You told him that?'

'Yes—and I reminded him of what he said on the night Christopher died. That we both want what's best for you. And that I believe I am best for you. And that I wasn't asking his permission to marry you—I wanted his blessing.'

'Oh!' Rachel breathed.

'Then he took me into the dining room and said, "Put wood in 't 'ole, lad". What does that even mean?'

'Shut the door.' Rachel smiled at his terrible northern accent.

'Well, I did shut the door, and your dad asked if I had a ring. I said we'd choose one together, but he said that you might want this…'

He took out a ring—a gorgeous pink ruby surrounded by little diamonds. It was a ring that Rachel had loved all her life.

'It's Mum's ring.'

'Yes.'

'I remember it,' she said.

It had glinted in the bedside light as her

mum had turned the pages of her bedtime stories. She could remember her smiles, and the scent of her perfume, and she wasn't scared to share those memories with him any more.

'Will it hurt too much to wear it?' Dominic asked. 'Because if that's the case...?'

'No, no,' Rachel said. 'I absolutely love it.'

'You really do have beautiful hands,' Dominic said as he slid the ring onto her finger.

And they were even more so now, with the perfect ring on them.

He kissed her then—a slow lingering kiss that tasted of patience rewarded and a very deep love.

He took the little bow that tied her dress and undid it, sliding his warm hands inside. His kiss was still tender as he undressed her and then pushed her back onto *their* bed.

As she lay watching him undress, she felt choked up, especially when he climbed into bed and held her. Because she knew how lucky they were to have been given this second chance.

'I'm sorry for all the hurt,' Rachel said,

and she knew the part she had played in their demise.

'No more saying sorry about that,' Dominic said. 'Maybe we were too young for a love this big?'

He kissed her again, and now it was more consuming, with the roughness of his jaw and the weight of his naked body warming hers.

He kissed her slowly all over, his mouth tasting her, pinking her skin and making her burn all over, burying himself in her, discovering her all over again.

And when she came to his lips, nothing could stop him. No sheath, no barriers. They were together again.

He drove into her with such passion, and she met him with the same force, until they were moving together, loving each other. And then she looked up and saw those velvet brown eyes closing as he lost himself in her.

They were locked in rhythm, with no secrets between them, no feelings unshared and no needs unmet…just her building moans that made him move faster and faster.

Then Dominic opened his eyes and watched

the delicious frenzy of her climax as she unravelled beneath him and he spilled into her.

And then there they lay, facing each other again, her hair back to curly, his eyes back to kind.

Lovers and loving each other all over again.

CHAPTER THIRTEEN

'IT'S *YOUR* WEDDING DAY?'

The hairdresser gaped in surprise at the calmest bride in the world, sitting in her chair.

Rachel deliberately hadn't gone to the place she'd once worked, because their wedding was a secret and just about them.

'Yes.' Rachel smiled.

'But you booked a "hair up for a wedding..." Usually brides like to have a trial...'

No trial had been necessary.

There was to be no family this time.

No pregnancy either—although Dominic was working on that!

No pressure.

The sun was bright and shining high as they met at a quarter to eleven outside the Town Hall.

It was a gorgeous listed building and there were people milling around outside, a newly married couple stepping out to the sound of cheers.

'I can't wait to marry you again,' Dominic said. 'You look beautiful.'

Rachel wore a flowery dress from a high street store and some wedge sandals for the occasion. Her red hair was curly and piled high and she carried a bunch of sunflowers—because they made her feel happy.

Dominic looked completely immaculate, of course. He wore a dark grey suit, a white shirt, a silver tie and a smile. He'd had his hair cut and gone for a hot towel shave. She could not wait to get her hands on that smooth jaw. In fact, she ran her hands over it and moved in for a kiss.

'Not until we're married, cheeky,' he said, and then offered his arm.

Together they walked in.

Their register office wedding was a very tiny one, because with two witnesses pulled at random from the street, they held hands and looked only at each other as the registrar spoke.

'The purpose of marriage is that you may always love, care for and support each other, through all the joys and sorrows of life. It is a partnership in which two people can pledge their love and commitment to each other; a solemn union providing love, friendship, help and comfort to you both through your life together...'

Hearing those beautiful words, Rachel started to cry. They had been here before, had heard those words before, but this time there was such certainty in the air that it was for ever, and it made the words sound extra-poignant.

'We know we can do this now,' Dominic said gently. 'Whatever life brings.'

She nodded and they made their vows, and she smiled as his ring slipped back on her finger, where it belonged.

And then her ring was back on his. And finally they were husband and wife again. And Dominic kissed the woman who was clearly destined to be his bride.

There were people everywhere as they stepped out of the small ceremony room. Love was in the air, and there were kissing couples and gorgeous bridesmaids trotting past as they were offered congratulations by people they didn't know. It was, for both of them, the most perfect wedding.

Rachel felt as if her heart might burst with happiness as they stood on the gorgeous staircase inside the Town Hall, with its crimson carpet and ornate banister, and had photos taken on their phones by a passing stranger. Especially when she felt Dominic's arm holding her tightly and she turned and saw his proud and confident smile as the moment was captured for ever.

They sent a photo to both sets of parents and some close friends to announce their union to the world.

'Your dad will be annoyed at missing out on a chance to party,' Dominic warned her.

'I'm sure he'll have a little party in our absence tonight, and we can head over tomorrow with a cake. Anyway, it's his turn next.'

They would be back at the Town Hall in precisely two weeks, for the wedding of her father and Moira.

Dominic had been right to tell Rachel to give Moira a chance, for her father too had found love again, and Rachel could not be more thrilled for him. She was starting to adore her new stepmother—this woman who was willing to reach for her coat rather than sit quietly by and be shut out of their family.

At last Dr and Mrs Hadley walked out of the Town Hall and into a taxi, to go for a very special wedding breakfast.

'This is my favourite place in the world,' Rachel told him as they walked in the gorgeous grounds of Chatsworth House and looked at the cascade of water in the fountains. Then, when they had selected their picnic spot, Dominic took out a bottle of champagne.

'Here's to us,' he said as they clinked glasses.

It felt so right to wear his ring, and so pleasurably strange to see Dominic wearing hers again.

But Dominic really was a lightweight, because one glass of champagne in, he was making her laugh as he stood up and ran across Capability Brown's perfectly manicured grounds. He started to spin like Maria in *The Sound of Music*, and she joined in, and they spun till they were dizzy, and then, the best part of all, they lay together on the grass and looked up to the bright blue sky.

'I'm sorry I never gave Sheffield a chance,' said Dominic. But he was more than happy to do so now, as he put on his terrible accent. 'I might even have gravy on me chips tonight.'

They were delirious with love, messing about on the lawn like the two teenagers they'd once been, and then lying back and relishing the fact that they were husband and wife.

Rachel sighed. 'I love it here.'

'I know you do,' Dominic said. 'Are you sure about us staying in London?'

'I'm very sure.' Rachel nodded. 'I like working at The Primary.'

May had been thrilled to have her back—and, of course, despite refusing to give Dominic her phone number, she'd had no problem in sharing the juicy gossip that Dominic and Rachel had once been husband and wife.

Rachel didn't mind. It had given people the heads-up about their relationship, so she didn't have to tell everyone, and even Tara had managed a smile and offered congratulations when they'd gone back.

'We'll be back up here often,' Dominic said now. 'We've got the flat, remember?'

It was their wedding present to each other. The little flat where they had started married life the first time around would be their heavenly escape when they came back to visit her family.

But for now it was on to Bakewell in the Peak District, where they had rented a gorgeous little honeymoon cottage, nestled in clouds of soft heather on the wild moors. There were low wooden beams and a log burner, and a welcome basket of food that they would explore later.

It felt as if it were just the two of them alone in the world, save for the sheep, and Rachel enjoyed a feeling of peace she had long forgotten—a sensation of utter contentment that wrapped around her like a hug. Dominic made her smile, but he also allowed her to cry and express all the emotions in between.

There was grass on his suit from where they had lain on the ground, and she felt the eternal thrill of Dominic as he took her in his arms and kissed his bride again.

'So... Are you happy?' Dominic asked the same question he had on the day she'd returned to his life.

And she knew he asked because it would always matter to him.

For Rachel there was no need to pause or examine her answer this time. 'So very happy.'

For she was back with the man she had always loved.

EPILOGUE

NIGHT FEEDS WERE the best.

Rachel loved nothing more than to sit in semi-darkness and just relish the quiet time with their little girl.

Araminta Aoife Hadley.

Minty.

'Minty?' her dad had barked when he'd come to visit them at the hospital. 'Oh, I've lived too long—I really have. First there's Pixie and now Minty. I'll be laughed out of the pub!'

'Oh, give it a rest, Dave,' Moira had said, and she and Rachel had shared a smile.

And then Rachel had teared up as she'd watched her dad holding little Minty, telling her just how very precious and loved she was.

Dominic's parents had visited too, and agreed she was beautiful indeed, and Dominic had had to borrow Rachel's superpower to push down his resentment as he'd accepted their congratulations and smiles.

Minty was now six weeks old, and while Rachel's pregnancy had been terrifying, she and Dominic had faced it together this time, sharing their hopes and fears and taking it in turns to be strong.

She had silky dark hair, a sweet rosebud mouth, fat cheeks and long fingers, and Rachel took her time to trace them all as she fed her. Her feet poked out from the little sleep suit and Rachel could not resist counting her tiny toes.

She was rather certain that Minty smiled.

When she'd finished feeding, instead of heading straight up the stairs, Rachel stood and cuddled her for a moment, rocking her as she held her, enjoying the sweet, milky baby scent and the softness of her hair as she gently paced the room before coming to stand at the fireplace.

They had, as both she and Dominic as well as all their visitors agreed, the best mantelpiece in the whole world.

At one end there was a photo of them on the steps at Sheffield Town Hall, both smiling—Dominic probably in terror and Rachel trying to contain her love.

At the other end there they stood again, thirteen years older and a whole lot surer of their mutual love.

And between them there were photos of Minty, and of Jordan and Heather's newest son, Andrew, who was Rachel and Dominic's godchild.

Richard's wife, Freya, was expecting again, so there might be another photo to add soon.

And there was Pixie, and her other nieces and nephews too. And there, nestled within the other photos, next to the beautiful portrait of her mother, the much-mourned Aoife Walker, with her gorgeous red hair and smiling eyes, was Christopher, in the arms of his parents.

They were both a part of their journey and a part of their family, and would be for evermore.

'If you throw me out I'll come back,' Dominic said, and his delightfully tricky wife smiled as she realised he had come downstairs to join her. 'And then we can get another wedding photo to put in the middle—because I'm just going to keep on marrying you.'

'And I'll just keep on saying *I do*.'

Rachel smiled, and when he held out his arms she handed him little Minty.

They were, they both knew, simply meant to be.

* * * * *

LET'S TALK
Romance

For exclusive extracts, competitions and special offers, find us online:

facebook.com/millsandboon

@millsandboonuk

@millsandboon

Or get in touch on 0844 844 1351*

For all the latest titles coming soon, visit millsandboon.co.uk/nextmonth

*Calls cost 7p per minute plus your phone company's price per minute access charge